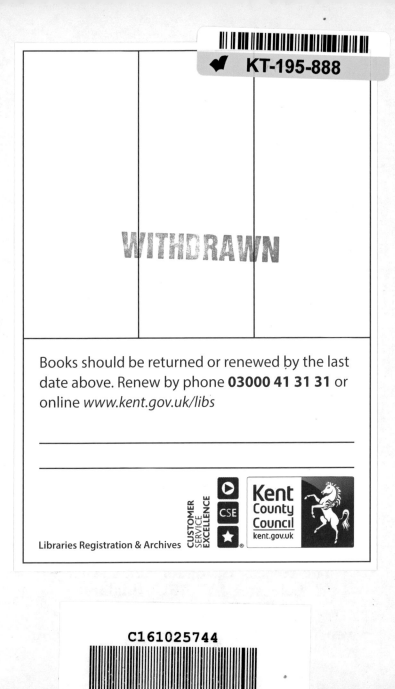

DIG TWO GRAVES

When the town's newspaper office is burned to the ground and the owner murdered, suspicion falls on Lane Cutler, the young deputy marshal of Progress. His alibi — that he was being held prisoner by ruffians at the time of the killing — persuades veteran lawman Ben McCabe to go in search of the truth. But the marshal runs into a wall of silence, shored up by blackmail and revenge. And when death strikes again, McCabe must join forces with a stranger before the final showdown . . .

PETER WILSON

◆

DIG TWO GRAVES

Complete and Unabridged

LINFORD
Leicester

First published in Great Britain in 2014 by
Robert Hale Limited
London

First Linford Edition
published 2016
by arrangement with
Robert Hale Limited
London

A catalogue record for this book is available
from the British Library.

ISBN 978–1–4448–2719–4

Published by
F. A. Thorpe (Publishing)
Anstey, Leicestershire

Set by Words & Graphics Ltd.
Anstey, Leicestershire
Printed and bound in Great Britain by
T. J. International Ltd., Padstow, Cornwall

This book is printed on acid-free paper

1

The plume of black smoke rose high into the night sky. At its base the flames crackled and spat, ripping through the wooden framework of the building that had been the town's newspaper office.

The large board that announced its title — *The Progress Leader* — tilted, then fell from its stanchion on the rooftop, crashing to the street.

They had come from all corners of town — a chain of willing hands eager to help the town's regular firefighters. Together they battled to save what was left of the building but two men took no part in the struggle to extinguish the blaze. Instead, they stood back in the shadows and smiled grimly as they watched the fire spread and strengthen its hold, destroying the evidence that would have condemned them to the hangman's noose.

Ben McCabe poured himself another whiskey, stared at the amber liquid and then raised his glass in front of the wide saloon-bar mirror. He offered a silent toast to his reflection.

The marshal of Progress County was in a nostalgic mood. He studied the face staring back at him: lined features, full head of dark hair greying at the temples, thicker around the chin than in his prime. McCabe was in his forty-third year, almost the veteran stage for a man who had spent nearly half of his life wearing a lawman's badge. The years had not been too unkind although the cold winters served to remind him of the wounds that he had suffered in the name of the law.

He remembered the time he had been left for dead in a Wyoming creek, rescued by the Kane family. And he could still recall with some satisfaction how he had managed to repay the debt by saving young Tommy Kane from the gallows after the boy had been wrongly convicted of murdering his friend.

It had been the start of a long-distance friendship and when Tommy wrote to him to say that he was giving up the life on a farm to study law with the idea of becoming a US marshal, Ben had felt a glow of pride. He knew Tommy would make a good lawman and Ellie Jacobs, the doctor's daughter who had become Mrs Kane, would be the perfect lawman's wife: something Ben McCabe had never experienced.

There had never been a Mrs McCabe although he had fond memories of Elspeth Kane, who had nursed him back to health, and ranch owner Mollie Cooper. Both women had briefly monopolized his affections.

But those days were behind him. Five years had passed since he attended the wedding of Tommy Kane and the pretty Ellie Jacobs and said farewell to the Kanes. His only contact with the family had been the occasional letter after he made his way back into Kansas and on to Progress County, a quiet, out-of-the-way town in need of a peace officer in the unlikely event of an outbreak of lawlessness.

McCabe had been ready for a life in semi-retirement: a fifty-dollar-a-month job as town marshal, keeping the cells clean and sending Saturday-night drunks on their way. Things had changed in the post-war years. The horrors of the conflict had long faded and farmers and ranchers were now thriving in an age of peace. McCabe liked it that way. He was considering the idea of yet another whiskey when the batwings of the saloon swung open and Clem Wallis, one of the town's old-timers, burst into the room.

'Fire! Down at the newspaper office. It's ablaze!'

McCabe put down his glass and raced out into the street. Townsfolk were rushing from all directions, desperate to offer their help to the small group of firefighters at the scene. If they noticed, nobody paid any attention to the thin-faced man retreating into the shadows.

Marshal Ben McCabe stumbled over the burnt-out wreckage of the building that had been the newspaper office. All around him, curious onlookers, prying children and town mayor Luther Bush searched for anything that might offer a clue to the cause of the blaze the night before.

'Bad business, Marshal,' Bush muttered, kicking aside a pile of ash. 'Sam must have been working late and knocked over a lamp. A terrible accident.'

The lawman nodded. 'Seems likely. Sam Duncan was a good newspaperman. The town's going to miss him.'

'The town and me both,' the mayor agreed solemnly. 'He always backed me whenever it came to election time.'

McCabe wiped the sweat from his brow, replaced his hat and moved away from the still smouldering ashes. He had added his weight to the battle to stem the blaze the previous night but, like the rest, he had been driven back by the heat of the flames.

'Well, Mayor, I reckon there's a grieving widow I got to see.'

'She's being comforted down at the church house. My wife and the minister's sister's with her,' Bush told him.

The badly charred, hardly recognizable body of newspaper owner Sam Duncan had been removed from the debris and taken along the main street to the funeral parlour. McCabe was walking past the undertaker's window when the local doctor, Jonas Miller, emerged from the building. He appeared to be in a state of near panic.

He was breathless, his voice coming in short, sharp gasps.

'Marshal! I'm glad I caught you. I . . . there's something you should know.'

'Calm down, Doc. Say what you've got to say, but say it slow.'

The doctor gulped, gathered his breath and eventually blurted out his message.

'I reckon that fire was no accident, Marshal. And it sure didn't kill Sam

Duncan. He was shot. I just took the bullet out of his back.' He paused before adding, 'And I found this clasped in his charred fingers.'

He opened his palm and Ben stared down at a soot-stained silver star.

2

Sarah Duncan was an impressive woman, strong-willed, assured. But as she sat in the living room of the mayor's house she looked a shadow of the imposing figure who so often was the centre of attention on Progress County business occasions.

That was not the woman whom McCabe found on his visit. She was slumped forward in her chair, her tear-stained handkerchief gripped tightly in her long fingers. Her reddened eyes and sheet-white face were further evidence that Mrs Duncan had shed many tears.

'I'm really sorry about Sam, Mrs Duncan,' McCabe said, his voice full of genuine sympathy, 'and I don't want to trouble you at such a time.'

She nodded feebly and muttered her understanding.

'Do we know what happened, Mr

McCabe? How the fire started?'

Ben found himself struggling for words.

'We're not sure,' he said. 'It seems like Sam must have knocked over a lamp and set a few papers alight. The thing is, Mrs Duncan, I need to know why Sam was in the office so late at night. Was that normal?'

'I don't know much about the newspaper business, Marshal, but Sam had not been himself for the last few days.'

Ben waited for her to continue.

'He . . . he said he had something important to do, that he was meeting somebody and it would be late before he got home.'

'Did he say who he was meeting?'

She shook her head, but replied: 'He didn't tell me but we did have a caller earlier in the afternoon.'

'And who was that?'

'That's the strange thing, Marshal. I thought he was out of town on business for you. It was your young deputy, Lane

Cutler, and they were arguing over something.'

Ben said nothing. Instead he fingered the fire-damaged star in his shirt pocket. There was now no doubt that it belonged to the young man he was grooming to be his successor come the day when he eventually decided to hang up his guns and leave law enforcement to younger men.

But he was left to wonder: what was Lane Cutler doing in the newspaper office late at night? And, even worse, had he shot Sam Duncan and started the fire?

★　★　★

The small church at the end of Progress Main Street was filled with mourners for the funeral service of Sam Duncan. Preacher Joshua Crowe, his solemn deep voice holding the congregation's undivided attention, spoke in glowing tribute to a man of truth in a land and time of lies and deceit: a man for whom the name of Progress was ideal.

'He was a man who believed in Progress, a man who made this town his home after turning his back on a life of riches and fame as a city newspaperman back East. He brought his lovely wife Sarah to our small community to — to die in such terrible circumstances, to have his life's work destroyed.'

He paused, stared long and hard from his pulpit at the congregation, and then added: 'God works in mysterious ways, my friends, and as we gather here this sunny morning, Sam Duncan's death is indeed a mystery to all of us. In a few moments we will lay the earthly remains of our dear friend and neighbour in a resting place in the hallowed ground of our small church. Before that I would ask you to bow your heads in silent prayer and seek the Good Lord's assistance to help Mr McCabe to apprehend the perpetrator of this heinous crime.'

Ben McCabe stood at the back of the crowded church and bowed his head.

But, unlike the others, he was not praying for divine assistance. He was wondering what had happened to his deputy Lane Cutler, the young man whose soot-stained badge was now lodged in his shirt pocket.

★ ★ ★

There were three riders. The tall one, unshaven, hollow-cheeked and dark-eyed, was up front. He was a loose-limbed, languid horseman who smoked cheap cheroots.

At the rear was the Mexican who liked to think he was important: sombrero, drooping moustache, stained poncho and gaudy striped trousers all added to the image he wished to portray. Miguel Vicenzo liked to be noticed.

Between the two was a third rider. He was slumped forward, his head covered by a black hood, his wrists tightly bound and tied to the horn of his saddle.

Suddenly the front rider pulled his horse to a halt and signalled to the Mexican to come forward. He threw away the remains of his smoke, turned in his saddle and surveyed the sorry figure strapped to the chestnut.

They had reached a ridge.

'See that, Mex?' the tall man said, pointing towards the horizon.

Vicenzo removed his hat, wiped his sweat-soaked face with a stained kerchief and followed the direction of the pointing finger.

'*Sí*. It is a town. Just a town.'

The tall man sniggered.

'That ain't just any old town, Mex. That's Progress.'

'Ah!' Realization dawned on the dim-witted Mexican.

'That's right, my stupid *amigo*. Ah!'

'So this is as far as we go, yes?'

'Sure is, Mex. This is where we cut our man loose and let him find his own way home.'

The Mexican dismounted and walked slowly back to where the third horse was showing signs of exhaustion. He pulled a knife from his belt, cut through the ropes tying the hooded figure to his horse and dragged him from the saddle, giggling like a child as the man's knees buckled under him and he fell face forward into the dirt.

Vicenzo prodded him with his boot and sneered when the man gasped in pain; then he took the reins of the riderless horse.

'We go now?'

The tall man lit another cheroot. Slowly enjoying the long intake of smoke, he eyed the Mexican. He felt some pity for the squat figure in the poncho but not enough to cause him any doubts about what he had to do.

'Now here's the thing, *amigo*. I've got my orders and they include leaving our friend here to make his way home and then to get back to the Bar in a hurry.'

'So? I understand. We go now, Vince?'

'Not we, *amigo*. Me.'

Without another word, the man

whose name was Vince pulled out his six-gun and sent two bullets into the heart of the Mexican, who died without knowing the reason for his death.

The killer reholstered his gun and dismounted. After emptying the dead man's pockets of the few dollars he had been carrying he lifted the body into the saddle and tied the corpse tightly across the back of the horse before turning his attention to the man lying face down, his head still covered by the hood.

'It's your lucky day, mister. I'm riding out of here and I want you to take my Mexican friend into town and arrange for a nice burial and a few prayers.' He paused to light a fresh cheroot. 'And you can tell the undertaker to dig two graves and save one of them for you.'

He took another vicious kick at the man in the hood, then mounted his horse and rode away.

Lane Cutler lay still until the sound of hoofs had faded and there was only silence. Silence and pain. He struggled to his feet and painfully worked to untie the ropes that had bound his wrists during the long ride to the outskirts of Progress.

Pulling the hood from his head, he blinked furiously as his eyes tried to adjust to the daylight. Gradually his surroundings came into focus. The young deputy marshal felt physically sick. He had taken a serious beating at the hands of his captors; throughout the long ride he had been deprived of food and drink and now he had been abandoned on the outskirts of the town that had been his home for the past three years.

A few yards away the lifeless body of the Mexican was strapped to a palomino, while another horse roamed in search of something worth chewing.

Cutler dusted himself down but even that act only added to the excruciating pain that racked his body. Slowly he stumbled towards the grazing horse and, despite his suffering, eventually managed to climb into the saddle and turn towards the long slope that led into town, leading the dead Mexican. But it was the words of his torturer — the man the Mexican had called Vince — that ran through the young deputy's mind. What did he mean? *Dig two graves and save one for you.*

★ ★ ★

Every step the horse took brought searing pain through Lane's battered body and there were times when he felt as though his remaining strength was fading fast. Twice he lost his grip on the reins of the horse carrying the body of the Mexican and each time he had to dismount to retrieve the reluctant palomino before continuing the slow ride into Progress.

The main street was deserted and although he had no idea of the time of day the sun was still low on the eastern horizon, so he suspected that the stores, the school and the saloon were still not open for business.

He managed to reach just beyond the outskirts, close to the livery stable and bathrooms, when his will finally surrendered. He slipped slowly from the saddle and was oblivious of any pain when his body slammed into the dusty street and blackness engulfed him.

★ ★ ★

There were voices, distant at first but then closer. Indistinct yet vaguely familiar.

'He's in a bad way, Ben. He's been savagely beaten and if I'm any judge it was by somebody who really enjoyed what he was doing. He has broken ribs, a bad head injury and I can't begin to think what internal damage he's suffered.'

'But he will pull through, Doc?' The question was filled with alarm.

'I don't know, Ben. I reckon it's probably up to him now, and he's going to need some help from the Almighty.'

Ben? Ben who? Lane Cutler tried to

18

collect his senses but the pain was overwhelming and he eventually drifted back into unconsciousness.

Later, maybe hours — or days? — he was aware of another voice, female this time, warm, comforting. He opened his eyes; slowly the face came into focus. A pretty face. Young and pretty. Lucy. It was Lucy and although there were tears in her sky-blue eyes, she was smiling.

'Hello, handsome. Welcome back.'

He tried to speak but the words would not come. It was Lucy Blake. His sweetheart. He was still alive.

'I — I . . . ' he tried again but she pressed her fingers gently against his bloodied, swollen lips.

'Don't try to talk, Lane. The doc says you need plenty of rest.'

He made a vain effort to lift himself on to his elbow but immediately fell back on to the soft bed.

'I have to see the marshal. I have to explain what happened,' he stammered, but again he was beaten by an overwhelming weakness.

'All in good time, young man.' It was the voice of Doctor Miller. 'Ben McCabe will still be here when you are up and on your feet again.'

At that moment he felt that the marshal would have a long wait before he was back on his feet. It was almost a week later when Lane Cutler, young deputy marshal in the town of Progress, was fit enough to be told that he was a suspect in the murder of newspaper owner Sam Duncan.

3

'You can't believe I had anything to do with Sam's death, Ben! You can't.'

Ben McCabe studied the young man opposite him. They were seated in the only cell in Progress's small marshal's office and although the door was open wide the young deputy was officially under arrest.

'It doesn't really come down to what I think, Lane,' Ben said, trying to sound sympathetic. 'I've got to go with the evidence and that looks pretty bad.'

Young Lane shook his head.

'I don't understand, Ben. I swear to God, I don't understand.'

'Then I guess I ought to tell you and see what you say.' He reached inside his shirt pocket and produced the smoke-stained badge that had been taken from the fire at the newspaper office.

'This is your deputy's badge, Lane. It

was taken from Sam Duncan's hand the night he was found with a bullet in the back. How do you suppose it got there? On the same afternoon you visited Sam's house and — '

'I didn't, Ben. I was never there.' Lane almost screamed the denial.

'You were seen. Mrs Duncan saw you talking to Sam and he told her he had arranged to meet somebody at the office that night.'

'That wasn't me, Ben. I wasn't here, I swear it,' Lane protested.

McCabe wanted to believe his young deputy but there was a witness. And evidence. And he could not ignore what was in front of him.

*　*　*

Two days before the blaze Lane Cutler was feeling important. Ben McCabe had put him in charge of the office while he was out at the Benson ranch. It was the marshal's third visit to the Double-B spread in the past two weeks and was confirmation of what Lane had been told by one of the young ranch hands — that Ben was serious about turning in his badge and buying the Benson place.

Old George had been trying to sell the small ranch a couple of miles outside Progress ever since his wife and son had been killed by a gang of drunken drifters nearly a year ago. McCabe and his posse had eventually tracked down three of the killers and they had been hanged down in Wichita, but George Benson's heart was no longer in the beef business and he was eager to go back East if the chance came along.

It was only a matter of agreeing a price before Ben would hang up his guns and settle down to a rancher's life. That would leave Lane in the right place to take over as town marshal.

He was alone in the office, deep in thought about the future and how he would soon be throwing away his deputy badge and becoming the Progress town marshal, when the message came in.

Charlie Reed burst into the office, breathless from his run down from the telegraph office. Lane swung his feet off the desk and rose to meet his visitor.

'Hi, Charlie. What's the big rush?'

'It's for you, Lane,' the old man gasped. 'Urgent, it says.' Cutler snatched the paper from Charlie's outstretched hand and read the message.

> to lane cutler, progress marshal's office, urgent, mother ill. doc believes it is serious, come soon. alice.

Lane reread the message from his sister, then folded the paper and stuffed it into his shirt pocket.

'Thanks, Charlie.'

Lane slumped back into his chair and pulled the telegram out of his pocket. Urgent. Doctor thinks it is serious. Come soon.

He had not heard from Alice in more than a year and on that occasion it had also been bad news — the death of their grandfather.

24

Now their mother was in bad health. He would have to go to her. It was a two-day ride and with the marshal out of town he would have to leave the office unattended. He forced a half-smile at the idea of Progress, one of the quietest, most law-abiding towns in the whole of Kansas, being without a peace officer for more than a couple of hours.

It was not yet midday, but he knew that Ben would be back by the middle of the afternoon so leaving the office unmanned for two or three hours was not going to put the town in any jeopardy. In the time since he had been installed as Ben McCabe's deputy there had been nothing more serious to deal with than the occasional barroom brawl or petty pilfering, so the chances of a crime outbreak in the next few hours were pretty remote.

He pulled his hat from its hook behind the door, buckled on his gunbelt and stepped out into the hot sun. It would be a hard, long ride — at least a two-day trip if he did not overstretch his young horse — so he stocked up with a few provisions before setting out on the ride north.

The young deputy rode steadily for three hours before arriving at a quiet, creekside glade that seemed the perfect setting for a break for both himself and his horse. He stretched his aching limbs and allowed his horse to graze near by and was splashing his face in the cooling creek water when he heard the sound. A snapping twig or the cocking of a six-gun? Whichever it was, Lane was in no position to do anything about it. His gunbelt lay on a rock several yards away and his horse, carrying his rifle in its sheath, was grazing lazily along the water's edge.

He got to his feet slowly and turned to find himself staring into the faces of two mounted men, both dark-skinned, unshaven — one of them a Mexican — and both pointing guns at his chest. Lane raised his arms.

'What do you want? You can see I ain't carrying.' He nodded towards his gunbelt on the rock.

'Lucky for you, *señor*.' The Mexican grinned, showing a row of broken but white teeth below his moustache. 'We do not wish to kill you.'

'Then what is it you want?'

The other man, tall, sour-faced, with thin, pointed features that could have been designed to display anger, dismounted and strode towards Lane.

'Keep him covered, Mex,' he ordered, reholstering his own six-gun.

'You Lane Cutler?'

Lane stood his ground as the man towered above him, their faces only inches apart.

'Who's asking?'

The tall man smirked, an ugly, twisted grin. 'Guess I am.'

Lane held the man's stare. A childlike cackle from the Mexican suggested that he was enjoying the moment.

'I'm Cutler.'

'Good,' the man said and turned away. It was a movement that caused Lane to relax — but too soon. Without warning, the tall stranger swung round and smashed his forearm so forcefully into the young lawman's jaw that he was sent spinning backwards. He fell into the creek.

Spluttering, he scrambled to his feet and tasted blood.

'Then you're the one we're looking for,' his attacker said as Lane struggled to climb out of the water. He never made it. Before he could make dry land the big stranger drew his pistol and smashed it across Lane's jaw. Blackness immediately swallowed him up as he hit the ice-cold water for a second time.

* * *

The pain was unbearable and his left eye remained closed. His wrists and ankles were bound tightly and despite the darkness he realized that he had been stripped of his shirt and pants. He tried to focus on his surroundings — a dark, damp cabin was his best guess, although the only light came from outside, through the gaps in an ill-fitting door.

Then there were voices, far off at first but getting closer.

The door opened and another stranger, older than the others with a neatly trimmed grey beard and long grey hair and needing the help of a stick to stand upright, entered. He was dressed in a brown town suit, complete with vest and high-collared shirt — the last type of man Lane expected to see.

'Mr Cutler,' he said in a voice that had been educated somewhere far away from the ranges of Kansas. 'I hope my men have not made you too uncomfortable, though I can see from your present state that you're not a willing visitor.'

Lane tried to speak but his swollen lips and jaw allowed only an incomprehensible mumble to escape.

The man in the suit continued: 'I realize you must be wondering why you were brought here and whether you will ever get out alive. Let me put your mind at rest. In a day or two — three at the most — you will be allowed to return to Progress, perhaps a little worse for your experience and with a bit of explaining to do to your marshal, Mr McCabe, but you will be alive. By that time my men will have finished the task I have set them and the rest . . . well that will be up to the law.

'Meanwhile I will order my men to make sure that you are treated rather more kindly than you have been so far. You will be fed and watered regularly and your clothes will be returned. Unfortunately you will have to stay here under guard until the time comes.'

He turned to leave but stopped in the doorway.

'One more thing, Mr Cutler. I don't want you to worry about your mother's state of health. That was purely a fabrication on my part to make certain that you were exactly where I wanted you to be at the right time. Your mother's health is fine — so far as I know. Goodbye, Mr Cutler. I don't expect we will meet again.'

He left the cabin, locking the door behind him and leaving Lane in the darkness, his brain still searching for an answer to the questions: why had he been brought here and what did a well-groomed city gent want with him? He fell into a fitful sleep only to be awakened when the door was sprung open and the Mexican stood in the morning sunlight. He was carrying a coffee mug and a plate of eggs and bacon.

'Good morning, *señor*. The boss says you have to be fed so I am here.'

'The boss? Who is the boss? And where is he?'

The Mexican grinned. 'Oh, he's not here. He is back at big house. He just says be sure that the man in the cabin is fed for two days.'

The Mexican knelt and placed the coffee and food on the cabin floor and turned to leave.

'Hold it, Mex. How am I supposed to eat with my hands tied?'

The Mexican chuckled. 'Not my problem, *señor*.'

He started to leave but turned
suddenly, a wide grin on his face.

'Only joking, my friend. But I warn
you. Outside is the big man, Vince, and
he is not friendly like me. He would like
very much to do much more of that to
you.' He pointed to Lane's bruised and
swollen features. 'And when I ask him
why, he tells me, 'I have my reasons,
Mex and they don't concern you.' So I
think you should not try to escape.'

He untied the ropes and Lane rubbed
his wrists in an attempt to restore some
circulation. He pointed to his ankles.

The Mexican cackled. 'You do not
eat with your toes, *señor*. And remember what I say about trying to escape.
Vince is a vicious man.'

Lane picked up the coffee mug and
the plate of bacon and eggs. He did not
know how long it had been since he'd
last eaten, but the hunger pains were a
strong reminder that it had not been for
some time.

The Mexican sat cross-legged on the floor opposite, smoking a foul-smelling cheroot. He was the compulsive talkative type, but nothing more than the hired help on the lowest rung of the ladder. He answered Lane's questions but told him nothing other than that the boss was at the big house and Vince was outside.

'Why am I here?' Lane asked, mopping up the remains of his breakfast with the last of his bread. The question brought another cackle from the Mexican.

'*Señor*, they tell me nothing so I know nothing. They just say, Miguel do this, Mex do that, so I do it. They say, Miguel, you go with Vince and bring back Lane Cutler, a young deputy marshal from Progress. So — I go and here you are. Maybe you upset the big boss, I don't know.'

'I don't even know who the big boss is,' Lane protested but his jailer simply shrugged and retied the ropes on the younger man's wrists.

'Maybe I ask,' he said, checking the strength of the knots.

A minute later Lane was left alone with his darkest of thoughts and fears.

The visits became regular; a hot stew and more coffee constituted the main meal and, despite his predicament, Lane was beginning to feel human again. But the Mexican clearly had his orders to say nothing about the reasons for the capture or the man behind it.

On his fifth visit the Mexican was not alone. Instead he was accompanied by the man who had been wearing the brown suit — this time he wore a more austere black — and the tall man with the long, stringy hair whom Lane now knew to be Vince. It was Vince who hurled a bundle through the open door.

'Your clothes, Mr Cutler,' the man in black said. 'I said I did not expect us to meet again but I feel I should say my farewells. It's time for you to leave us.'

'Cut him free, Mex,' Vince snapped. 'And be quick about it. We got some riding to do.'

'My men will see you safely home,' the boss man said, 'and if you are wondering why, then take my advice. Go along quietly. Vince here has quite a temper if he is riled and I see your bruises are healing quite well.'

They watched while Lane pulled on his pants and boots and fastened his red shirt before the Mexican retied his hands.

'Oh, and there is just one more caution, Mr Cutler. I'm sure you will understand that we don't want your marshal or your friends in Progress to come looking for us.'

From behind, the Mexican threw a hood over Lane's head. He was still tying the string when the full force of a vicious punch in the stomach knocked the wind out of his body. He doubled up in pain but before he could recover another blow to the face was followed by another, then another. And the darkness of the hood became the blackness of unconsciousness.

He was still only semi-conscious

when the man called Vince put a bullet in the unfortunate Mexican and left Lane Cutler to ride into Progress with the message: *dig two graves*.

* * *

'And that's God's honest truth, Ben,' Lane said. 'That's exactly what happened.'

Ben McCabe had listened to his deputy's story without interruption, but now he was staring out of the office window, his back to Lane Cutler. Out in the street the good folk of Progress were going about their daily business, unaware that their popular young lawman was behind the bars of his own jail cell pleading his innocence to the one man he felt he could trust and who would believe in him.

McCabe turned away from the window and sank into his desk chair. He looked through the open cell door at the young man on the bunk. He wanted to believe Lane's story but he had a strange feeling that he wasn't being told everything.

'I believe you, Lane,' he said without conviction, 'but the question is: will a judge feel the same?'

'But I'm innocent, Ben. Why would I want to kill Sam Duncan?'

A good question, Ben thought. But, almost as puzzling was why would somebody else set him up for murder? If Cutler was innocent, the real killer was determined to see the young lawman hang for the crime. Who? And why?

'Like I said, son,' Ben told him, 'even though I may believe you, the evidence is stacked against you. Your badge was found in Sam Duncan's hand. You were seen talking to Sam only a few hours before he was killed and you tell me you weren't even in town; you say you were being held prisoner but you don't know where.'

'But the telegraph message, Ben! Charlie brought it to tell me that my mother was sick and I was to come quick.'

Ben got to his feet. 'The problem is, Lane, we can't get Charlie to confirm that. He retired two days ago and left town to join his grandchildren out on the coast.'

Lane slumped forward and stared at his feet. 'God, Ben. What's happening? I — I'm scared.'

McCabe said nothing. Things looked bad for his assistant but this was not the first time he had found himself in a position where he had to save a young friend from the noose.

Back in the days when he was a US deputy marshal it had been to repay a debt to the Kane family, who had nursed him back to health after he had been left for dead. Young Tommy Kane had been found guilty of killing his best friend after an argument over a girl who was now Tommy's wife.

The difference was that on that occasion he was certain of Tommy Kane's innocence. This time he was not so sure that Lane Cutler was telling him the whole truth. He had been held prisoner but he did not know where or by whom — just a Mexican who was now dead, a thin, lank-haired man called Vince and a well-dressed, well-spoken man who used a stick to assist him.

Eventually he came to a decision.

'I guess I'll just have to keep you locked up while I try to find out the truth about what has happened. I'll hold off from sending for the circuit judge for a day or two. Meantime, if you remember anything you think might help, then I'd sure be happy to hear it.'

Lane looked forlorn as he sat on his bunk.

'There's just one thing, Ben. I don't know if it means much but before Vince killed the Mexican he talked of some place called the Bar.'

'The Bar? You sure?'

Lane nodded.

'Maybe it does mean something, maybe not,' Ben said quietly, locking the cell door. 'But you got my promise,

Lane. If you're telling me the truth I'll do everything I can to clear your name and find out who killed Sam Duncan. If you're lying, I'll see you hang.'

With that he walked out of the office and headed for the Duncan house. He had made his promise to Lane Cutler but it was as much a promise to himself. It was something he had to do before he finally put his money into the Benson spread and left law and order to younger men.

4

Ben McCabe made his way past the burnt-out ruins that had once been a prospering newspaper office. He paused only briefly to examine the scene of Sam Duncan's murder. Could Lane Cutler, a fresh-faced budding lawman, have murdered the owner of the *Progress Leader*? If so — why? And was his claim that he had received a message from his sister that his mother was seriously ill the truth? He now said that the message was nothing more than a trick to lure him away from town.

Ben wanted to believe his deputy, the man who would be following him as town marshal once the deal for the George Benson spread had been finalized. It was a mystery he was determined to solve before he eventually handed in his badge for the last time.

A stray dog snapping at his feet and

41

then running off brought his thoughts back to the present. He knew he had to start his investigations somewhere — his early career as a railroad special agent had taught him not to take things at face value. The home of Sam Duncan's widow seemed as good a place as any to start.

★ ★ ★

Sarah Duncan appeared to be bearing up well to the loss of her husband and she even offered a welcoming smile when she opened the door to Ben's knock.

'Come in, Marshal,' she said pleasantly. 'I've kind of been expecting you.'

He removed his hat and followed her into the small, neatly furnished house.

Mrs Duncan had been a strikingly attractive woman in her younger days and many of the good folk of Progress were of the opinion that Sam Duncan had got the better end of the bargain when the couple married. Rumour also had it — though it was never confirmed

— that it was Sarah's family money that had enabled Sam to establish the *Progress Leader* when he arrived in town with a view to setting up the paper.

But no sooner had he started to print the *Leader* than the call came from his old Chicago newspaper to act as its correspondent in the war.

The wounds that Sam Duncan had suffered at the hands of the rebels were no worse than those suffered by thousands of other soldiers on both sides, but he arrived back in Progress a hero of the conflict. But, also like soldiers of both sides, the war had changed him. Gone was the friendly, carefree Sam Duncan who had set up the paper, and in his place came a man scarred by the brutality of too many battles and too much bloodshed.

'The war couldn't kill Sam but it killed his soul,' the Reverend Joshua Crowe explained to Ben when the new marshal arrived in town.

Ben had never known the pre-war

Sam but he always found the version he did know to be friendly enough without ever hinting that he had once been the life and soul of any party.

And he did take some pride in his newspaper. It had supported Ben's appointment and his planned reforms in law enforcement, such as the order to surrender sidearms to all saloon keepers and a clampdown on drunkenness.

'Progress is not a frontier town and we don't intend to become one, thanks to our new marshal, Ben McCabe,' had been Sam Duncan's rallying call under the heading: DRUNKS AND GUNSLINGERS NOT WELCOME IN TOWN. PROGRESS IS NOT JUST A WORD. IT MEANS WHAT IT SAYS.

Mrs Duncan showed Ben through to a small, comfortable sitting room at the side of the house. Beyond the window was a neatly trimmed garden plot complete with an attractive flowerbed — her pride and joy — and the whole place had a charm that Ben had not known since his boyhood days.

'You say you were expecting me, Mrs Duncan?' Ben said, settling into an armchair.

'Sarah, Marshal McCabe, please. Well, I heard you have arrested your young deputy for Sam's murder. I thought maybe you would be stopping by to let me know.'

Progress was a small town and it did not take long for news to reach almost everybody who lived in the area.

'That's true,' Ben told her, 'but Lane says he didn't do it, Sarah,' he emphasized her name in the hope that it would put her at ease, 'and I suppose I've got a duty to look into what he has been saying.'

'Of course, Marshal.' Mrs Duncan nodded. 'It's only right, but I don't know how I can be much help to you.'

'I'm not sure either but . . . there are just one or two things to clear up before the circuit judge comes to town.

'You said Sam told you he had arranged to meet somebody at the office that night and you think it was Lane. You saw him talking to your husband that afternoon.'

'That's right, Marshal. I was upstairs dusting the room when Sam had a visitor.'

'And that was Lane?'

'I saw him clear as day. I looked out of the window and they were talking in the garden below.'

Ben spun his hat on his fist, a habit he had developed when he was preparing to ask a question that wouldn't be liked.

'You're sure it was Lane?'

Sarah Duncan stiffened.

'Who else could it have been, Marshal?' she said testily. 'He was wearing that red shirt with its black shoulders and that battered Stetson he's so proud of. Oh, it was young Cutler all right, and that's what I'll be telling the judge when the time comes.'

Undeterred by Mrs Duncan's sudden change of attitude, Ben pushed on: 'But you didn't see his face?'

'Like I said, I was upstairs, so I was looking down on them talking.'

'What did Sam say when he came in? Did he say it was Lane he had been talking to?'

'No, just that he had arranged a meeting at the office. Look, Mr McCabe, I don't know what you want me to say or what that young man has been telling you. Lane Cutler may be a friend of yours, he may even be a good deputy marshal, but my husband is dead and as far as I could see it was Lane who killed him. His badge was found in Sam's hand.' She stood up suddenly and said: 'Now, if that don't fit in with your thinking, I'm sorry, but I've got nothing more to say.'

Ben knew he would find no further help at the Duncan house. He nodded his thanks and left. Lane had told him how he had been held captive and stripped of his clothes, so Sarah Duncan's identification of her husband's mystery visitor was proof of nothing.

All she had seen were the clothes

— red shirt, battered Stetson — not who was wearing them. And there was still the question: why would a young, ambitious lawman in line to become town marshal kill a local newspaper owner?

Ben was closing the garden picket-gate when he almost bumped into Mrs Duncan's next visitor, Progress mayor Luther Bush. McCabe waited for the mayor to approach.

'Good to see you, Luther. It saves me a long walk to your house.'

Bush offered his public smile and extended his hand.

'Good morning, Ben. I take it you've just been to see Mrs Duncan. How is she?'

'She's fine, Mayor. And she's sure that it was Lane who killed her husband.'

'And you aren't?'

'Lane says he didn't do it and I think I believe him. Why would he kill Sam? There's no reason.'

The mayor was silent for a moment.

Then he said: 'Maybe we ought to talk, Ben.'

Luther Bush had arrived in town more than twenty years earlier, a young man flush with riches. He had done as much as anybody to turn Progress from a one-street settlement of drifters into a bustling town. Now a burly, red-faced man in his late fifties, Bush's history had remained a closed book to the people of Progress, but he was the man who had been the driving force for the place to live up to its name after the local elders had elected him the first mayor. Many years later he had recommended Ben's appointment as town marshal, having heard of his career as a lawman: railroad detective, small-town sheriff and US deputy marshal. But they had never become close friends. Theirs was a business arrangement and that suited both men, although when Bush rebuilt the town's first hotel, where he had stayed on his arrival, and alongside it now was his Regal Palace saloon and gambling hall, he gladly offered the marshal the use of a room. He later added the Silver Spur to his business interests.

'I like the idea of having the law close at hand,' Bush had said at the time, but Ben had to remind him that being mayor didn't entitle him to a personal police force.

The two men walked slowly away from the house and had almost reached the burnt-out newspaper office when the mayor spoke again.

'I wouldn't want Sarah to hear what I have to say, Marshal, but I have to be honest: Sam was not the man she would have everybody believe him to be.'

Ben waited for more. He could see that Luther Bush was far from comfortable with what he was about to say.

'Sam Duncan was a good friend of mine, Marshal; we had known each other a long time so it doesn't come easy to me to talk about him after what happened. Sarah is fooling herself.'

Again Ben said nothing. The mayor

was clearly anxious to impart information and was having trouble doing it. Was he about to betray his recently buried friend?

Eventually Ben forced himself to break the silence. 'What's on your mind, Mayor?'

'I can see you're not convinced about Lane being the killer — and if it's any help I think you might be right.'

'I've got him in the cell and to be honest, Luther, it doesn't look good for him,' Ben replied. 'There's the badge found in Sam's hand, the fact that Mrs Duncan insists it was Lane she saw talking to her husband and that he was missing for a couple of days. Yeah, things are looking bad, except . . . ' Ben paused.

'Except what, Marshal?'

'I can't see what reason Lane would have to kill Sam Duncan. His story is that he was on his way to visit his sick mother when he was attacked and held prisoner.

'He says his clothes were taken and he was watered and fed until they decided to release him. They gave him back his clothes, led him to the outskirts of town after beating him senseless.'

'And then they left him there to bring in that dead Mexican,' the mayor interrupted. 'That doesn't make any sense.'

'I reckon not, except that he was badly beaten and the doc reckoned he was lucky to live through it. Somebody did that to him.' Ben shook his head in bewilderment. 'So — what was it you were going to tell me?'

'Oh, maybe . . . Look, Ben, two days before he was killed Sam got drunk — seriously drunk — in my place. He was losing a lot of money and I tried to drag him away from the table. He got hostile, started to threaten anybody in range — including me — and he even turned on Laura, the woman who runs the Regal Palace for me. He was shouting and bawling and it took me all my strength to calm him down.

'I warned him that Sarah wouldn't like the idea of him losing money and drinking heavy but he just laughed in my face. 'But she ain't gonna find out, though, is she, Luther? I mean — who's goin' to tell her? You? I don't think so. Besides, she's still got enough to live on out of what her father gave us.'

'I couldn't keep him quiet, Marshal. And then he said something I didn't understand. He said: If I find myself short of a few bucks, I can always go to young Cutler. He owes me. And he'll go on paying as long as I have to tell him.'

'I asked him what he meant by that but all he would say was that it was between him and Cutler.'

'That was it?' Ben queried.

'Not exactly. He said if the money dried up I could always read about it in his newspaper. I didn't catch much else because he suddenly slumped into a drunken stupor. There was just one more word.'

'And what was that?'

'It was something I didn't understand. He said, 'Quillan'.'

★　★　★

53

Ben toyed with the food on his plate as he sat at a corner table in the small café that was his regular eating place. Carla, the young widow who owned the café, stood over him.

'My cooking not to your liking today, Mr McCabe?' There was more hurt than anger in the question.

Ben looked up absently. Carla Jack was a pretty woman, widowed too early in life when her husband came up against a gun who was quicker than he was. Ben had warned him often enough that such a man would come along one day. They would argue over a card or a drink or something just as trivial and they would fight and somebody would die. That was what happened when Billy Jack met Clay Bannister.

A fair fight — all the witnesses agreed. Billy was a hothead and if it had not been Bannister it would have been some other gun-happy drifter or a cowboy with a big reputation and a grievance to match.

Carla was left to bring up her young son — Billy Junior was not yet ten years old — and to run her small eating-house on the corner of Main Street.

'No, Carla, your cooking's fine as always,' Ben said. 'It's just I've got things on my mind.'

Carla slipped almost unnoticed into the chair opposite. 'Like to talk about it? It might help.'

Ben smiled. 'Thanks, Carla, but I think this is something I have got to work out for myself. I'm not sure you would want to hear about it.'

'You could always try me. I'm a good listener. Heck, I have to be with young Billy never knowing when it's time to stop talking.'

Ben tried another mouthful of pie, giving himself a bit more thinking time. Carla waited while he drank his coffee before she said, 'I expect you're worried about young Lane. Is that it?'

'That's right,' Ben said, suddenly eager to have somebody share his troubles. 'I've got the kid locked up for killing Sam Duncan.' He shook his head and snorted. 'I don't know why I keep thinking of him as a kid, he's twenty-one years of age, but I just don't think he did it. It doesn't make sense.'

He pushed the plate away more aggressively than he intended. He was surprised at Carla's reaction.

'You're probably right, Mr McCabe, it doesn't sound like something Lane would do, but then, if he *did*, he was doing some folk a favour.'

Ben's puzzled frown prompted her to carry on. 'Sam Duncan was not a nice man, Marshal.' She chuckled at that. 'Oh, I'm not saying that not being nice should be enough to get a man killed but . . . well, let's just say if Lane Cutler wanted Sam Duncan dead he wouldn't be alone.'

Barely an hour earlier Ben had heard from the town mayor that the newspaper owner was not the upright citizen that his wife and others believed him to be; that he had boasted about how Lane Cutler would finance his gambling and drinking. Now Carla Jack was also painting a darker picture of the murdered man.

'Tell me more,' Ben said encouragingly.

'It happened before you came to Progress, Marshal. Sam Duncan used to eat his meals here — especially when he had been working late at his newspaper; said it was not fair on Sarah for him to come home late demanding to have a meal on the table. So he came here.

'At first everything was fine and then he started to get familiar, making suggestions.

'He knew that Billy spent a lot of time out on the road — he sometimes rode shotgun on the mail stage. Anyways, Sam Duncan came in one night real drunk. Young Billy was upstairs asleep in his bed and Billy was across the street in the Palace — he liked to go there some nights for a hand of cards and a few drinks. I was clearing things away and was about to close up but Sam demanded something to eat. I told him it was too late and I was ready to lock up for the night. At first he just smiled and turned to leave but he had just reached the door when he turned round and leered at me. It was horrible. He said: 'If I can't have anything to eat, Carla, what can I have?' Before I could say anything he leapt at me. I didn't know what to do. I wanted to scream but he had his hand over my mouth. If I had been able to cry out I would probably have woken young Billy and he'd be frightened.

'With his free hand, he clawed at my clothes, ripping my dress away from the shoulder. I am no weakling, Mr McCabe. I fought and I scratched but I knew I was losing. He pushed me to the floor and fell on top of me. If he hadn't been so drunk I think I would have been . . . ' her voice faded at the memory, 'well, you know. But he was drunk and I somehow managed to find the strength to push him off. I lashed out with my knee and caught him where it hurt most. He let out a yell and cursed at me but he did not give up. He was on top of me again and I was ready for the worst

58

when there was a sudden smashing of glass. My husband had burst into the room. He grabbed Sam by the collar and dragged him away. He hauled him to his feet, threw him out of the shattered door and went after him.

'They were gone a long time and knowing Billy's temper I dreaded the worst. I was scared he might beat Sam to a pulp or pistol-whip him to death.

'I just sat against the counter curled up and frightened to move. Eventually Billy came back in and knelt down beside me. He could be very gentle when he wanted to be and he lifted me to my feet and put his arms around me.

' 'Easy, Carla,' he said, 'he's gone now — he won't be back.'

'I dreaded to ask the question but I couldn't stop myself. 'You haven't . . . ?'

' 'Killed him? No, he'll still be spreading his poison in that newspaper of his. He's a lucky man, Carla.'

' 'Lucky?'

' 'I guess I owe him — it's what kept him alive.'

' 'Owe him? What do you mean, Billy? What do you owe a man like Sam Duncan?'

'I never got an answer, but whatever it was, things were never the same again.'

Ben left the Little Lady café with a clearer picture of Sam Duncan, newspaper owner and respected member of the community. First Lane Cutler, now Carla Jack — even his friend Luther Bush — knew differently. Who else in the small town of Progress had reason to want Duncan out of the way?

It was a hot dry day with no cover from the early-afternoon sun when Ben went back to his office. Lane Cutler was in his cell, staring blankly out of the barred window, his plate of food still untouched on the bed.

Ben filled two mugs from the coffee pot on the stove and entered the cell.

'You ought to drink this and then we can talk, Lane,' he said, slumping on to the bed. 'And you can tell me what you know about Quillan.'

5

The war had been over for almost two years when Bob Cutler pulled his horse to a halt on a ridge overlooking the small farmhouse. He was tired, he had had enough of running and hiding. His days of looting and killing were ended. Quantrill and his raiders were either dead or locked away and Cutler was on his way home. William Quantrill himself was, long dead — shot by federal troops in Kentucky in the last year of the war; Jesse James and the Younger brothers had scattered and the rest had broken away to form their own bands of irregulars. Cutler had joined up with a small group of Kentuckians who had deserted Quantrill and had been on the run after the Lawrence massacre of 1863. There had been too many train robberies and killings and jailbreaks. And too many Wanted posters bearing a crude sketch of Bob Cutler and offering rewards ranging from $100 to $500 were pinned to the walls of the sheriffs' offices and trees across the territory.

There was a plume of smoke rising from the distant farmhouse and out front a youth was chopping wood. It had been almost five years since Bob Cutler left his home to join the army of the Confederacy but it had taken less than a year for him to realize that theirs was a losing cause and there were better pickings on the fringes of the battles, in sabotage and wrecking; opportunities that arose regularly in the company of the James and Younger brothers.

But now all that was behind him. Below, in the fertile valley he remembered, a few horses strolled around the corral, cattle chewed on a distant slope. But Cutler's eyes were focused on the young axe-wielding man near a broken-down wagon. Even from such a distance Cutler could see that much had changed in five years. The fresh-faced child he had left behind five years ago had grown and broadened, the short blond hair was now shoulder length. He paused as the youth broke from his work to mop his brow and help himself to a cup of water from a bucket. Then he dug his heels into the horse and began his descent towards his home.

★   ★   ★

Lane Cutler paused to wipe his face and help himself to a cup of water. It was getting towards midday but there was still work to be done before it was time to eat. But first there was the man high on the ridge. He was clearly watching the house and there were very few riders who passed this way. Lane put down his cup and walked slowly towards the house.

He had learned to become wary of strangers. The last caller to the homestead had been the sheriff of Redwood. He had not been a welcome visitor, bringing with him the news that Bob Cutler, Lane's and Alice's father and husband of Joanna, was wanted for murder. There was a reward of $500 for his capture dead or alive.

'There'll be bounty hunters calling, Mrs Cutler,' the lawman had told them, 'and, to be honest, there isn't much I can do about them. The law's on their side and . . . well, your husband is wanted for train robbery and murder.'

Dan Hayes, sheriff of Redwood and father of Lane's best friend, had left without a word of sympathy for the Cutler family, except to say that if Bob returned home they should let him know . . . for their own safety.

But the weeks had passed and nobody had come. Until now.

Lane reached the house and pulled the always-loaded rifle from behind the door. His mother looked up from her place at the kitchen table.

'What's wrong, Lane?'

'Maybe nothing, Ma, but — well it could be one of them bounty hunter fellers the sheriff told us about.'

Joanna got to her feet and hurried

across the room. 'That was months ago, Lane. Don't you think they'd have been here before now if they were coming?'

'The sheriff said we can't be too careful, Ma. I'm just being careful,' he said, gripping the rifle more tightly. 'Don't worry, I won't shoot unless I have to.'

He went back out on to the veranda. The rider had now reached the foot of the slope and was approaching at a slow, leisurely pace. He was certainly not a man in a hurry.

Young Lane studied the approaching figure — a thin-faced man, ill-shaven and dressed in old clothes and a hat he recognized as the same type that had been worn by the Confederate soldiers he had seen in Redwood. The rider had reached the corral when Lane stepped down from the veranda and raised his rifle.

'That's far enough, mister. What do you want?'

The man leaned forward on his saddle horn and smiled, a crooked sort of grin that did nothing to suggest he was on a friendly visit.

He pushed his hat away from his forehead and wiped his face with his kerchief.

'Hot day, son. A man could use a drink.' He dismounted and walked towards the well. 'You ain't gonna kill me over a cup of water, are you?'

Lane watched as the man slowly helped himself to a drink and then settled on the wall surrounding the well.

'What's your name, son?'

'None of your business, mister, just take your drink and move on.'

The man stood, threw the remains of his water into the dirt.

'I don't think that would be a good idea, Lane. I'm real sorry you didn't recognize me but five years is a long time in the life of a kid. What are you now? Fifteen? Sixteen years old? No, fifteen. That's right, ain't it?'

Lane said nothing.

'Hell, I should know — even if you don't know me. I'm your father, boy. I'm Bob Cutler. Back from the war.'

Lane kept his rifle steady. Was this man telling the truth? It was true, he did look vaguely familiar but he had been only ten years old when his father left home. He remembered it well enough, it was the day after his birthday, the day after the whole family — his elder sister Alice, himself and his mother and father — had visited Redwood for the marching-out parade as the local recruits left on their way to war. Was this the man who had been with them that day?

The answer came from behind him. He had not heard his mother come out of the house but she now stood at his shoulder.

'Lower your rifle, Lane. This man is your father.'

There was no warmth in the announcement, no rush to embrace the man who had suddenly and unexpectedly reentered her life after more than five years.

'You'd better come inside, Bob.' Joanna Cutler turned and walked back into the house and Lane lowered his rifle. Bob Cutler grinned at his son.

'The horse is tired, son. He needs a good rub down and a feed.' He slapped the horse's reins into Lane's hand and walked past him into the house. The boy watched the man who had become a stranger stride up the steps. He had dreamed of the day when his father would come home but this was not the reunion he had expected. He unsaddled the horse, filled a nosebag and reluctantly went inside to join his parents.

★ ★ ★

The days that followed Bob Cutler's return to his home were not the joyous occasion a family, reunited after a five-year separation, would have hoped for.

Cutler's attempts to win back the affections of his young son were restricted to tales of his wartime adventures, suitably doctored to enhance his heroism in the Confederate cause. He dismissed the Wanted posters as part of a plot to gain revenge on men who had done so much to damage the Union forces.

'But the war has been over for two years.' It was Joanna Cutler who spoke. 'Where have you been since then?'

Her husband rose from the table and walked purposefully across the room to where his wife was sitting close to the open fire.

'I already told you, Joanna. Yeah, I've been hiding out. I couldn't come home sooner.'

'Robbing and killing with the James gang.'

Bob Cutler slammed his fist down on to the table.

'Damn you!' he snapped. 'You don't know how it was. You didn't see men getting their arms blown off, or their guts torn out; you didn't see men getting blinded and butchered all because some crazy politicians had the idea that they knew what was best for everybody else. Yeah, I did a lot of bad things that you reckon I should be ashamed of. Well, let me tell you, I ain't ashamed. It happened and it's over and now I'm home to stay. So you,' he turned away to face Lane, 'and you will just have to get to like the idea.' He stormed out of the room, slamming the door behind him.

Bob Cutler's mood showed no signs of improving over the next few days and it was clear to Lane that his father was already hankering for a return to the days when he was free of the restraints and responsibilities of family life on a small farm.

The news that his daughter Alice had married and moved away two years earlier was another reason for his bitter mood and young Cutler knew after only a week that his father was a wild spirit and the day would soon come when he would be gone again.

It was on the eighth day that they came. Lane was exercising the horses and his father was making a lethargic attempt to restore a disused buggy into workable order when two riders appeared on the same northern ridge Cutler had used.

In the distance the riders paused, took in the scene below, before beginning their descent from the hilltop. It was when Cutler was taking a pause from his attempt to replace a wheel on the buggy that he spotted them. Instinct told him that this was not going to be a neighbourly call.

Bounty hunters. The kind who didn't ask questions, who believed their quarry should be strapped over the saddle of a horse and dumped at the door of the undertaker while they collected the reward on the Wanted bill. 'Dead or Alive' was an invitation to shoot first and talk later. Bob Cutler had known many such men — and now they had come for him.

Throwing down his hammer, he raced towards the house. He had been expecting this day to come soon and he was prepared. His horse, already saddled for a quick getaway, was grazing on the far side of the corral fence. Rushing up the steps, he burst into the house. Snatching his gunbelt and rifle from their place behind the door, he snapped at his startled wife:

'Get out and tell the kid to bring my horse out back. Hurry, woman — unless you want blood all over the house!'

Outside, Lane Cutler looked on in alarm as the two riders approached at increasing speed. Like his father, he knew these men were not coming to pay their respects.

What could he do? He was a fifteen-year-old boy who knew little of his father's life and liked even less. It was only when he heard his mother's voice — urgent, even desperate — screaming for the horse that he was spurred into action.

The riders were approaching fast but a rifle shot stopped them in their tracks. They dismounted and dashed for the cover offered by a disused barn.

After that it all happened so fast that Lane would barely remember it. An exchange of gunfire . . . a scream from one of the strangers . . . a cursed warning to his father . . . and then, somehow, the sight of his father riding out of his life for ever.

But that was not the end of it. Once inside the house, Lane knew that, whatever he thought of Bob Cutler, the man was his father and it was his duty to hold up the bounty hunters for as long as possible. Ignoring his mother's protests, Lane took his rifle down from the wall, and crouched by the window. He waited and was beginning to think that the two men had given up their quest when they suddenly appeared from behind the barn, shooting wildly towards the house. Lane fired back but aimed high and the bullet went harmlessly over their heads. Crouching, the two men weaved their way to their horses, remounted and, sitting low in the saddle, raced towards the house.

Lane felt himself trembling. He had never fired at a man before; rabbits and raccoons were all he had ever had in his sights. But this was different. These men were out to kill his father unless he stopped them.

Suddenly the riders veered off, one to the left, the other to the right, — and the young Cutler swung the rifle first one way, then the other, his finger hovering uncertainly over the trigger.

He was aware of his mother yelling at him to move away from the window but his head was spinning. And it caused him to hesitate a second too long, just enough time for the gunmen to make their way to the back of the house in pursuit of Bob Cutler. Lane got to his feet, raced past his mother and on to the rear veranda.

The retreating figure of his father was struggling up a distant slope but the gap between him and the men chasing was narrowing with every stride.

This time, Lane did not hesitate. Levelling his rifle, he fired at the right-hand rider. It was as though time had stood still as he crouched there on the steps of the veranda and he watched the man slump forward in his saddle. The other rider pulled up and turned to check on his partner before turning back to help. The mount of the apparently wounded man who was sitting almost doubled over the saddle horn was reduced to a walk.

Lane took aim and prepared to fire

again. But this time he didn't make it. Instead, his mother gripped his shoulder and spun him round.

'No, Lane! Stop.' It was almost a scream. 'Let them go! Your father's made his own life. It's the way he wanted it — I don't want to see my son going the same way!'

Lane lowered the rifle and slumped on to the top step. Of course, his mother was right: his father was no good. Wanted for murder and train robbery, he lived a life on the outside of the law and, in his heart, Lane knew that this would be how he would die, whether it was at the hands of the two bounty hunters now closing in on him, or at the end of a noose or by a lawman's bullet.

He stood up and watched his father disappear over the hill. He was safe for now but Lane put his arm around his mother and they went into the house.

★ ★ ★

Lane drained his coffee cup and paused in his story. Ben McCabe refilled the cup but said nothing.

'I was fifteen years old, Ben,' the young deputy said, a plea for sympathy in his tone. 'They wanted to kill my father.'

'Go on, Lane, tell me the rest. What happened after that?'

'The man I shot — he died. Two weeks later, when I was in the general store, I heard folk talking about a man who rode in with a bullet in his back. He was helped into the doc's by two men who were coming out of the saloon. One of them reckoned he knew who the man was and that he was a young rowdy. He died without saying anything but I knew he was the man I had shot. Seems he was only a couple of years older than me.'

Ben studied the young face of the boy killer. It was clear that, even after all this time — more than six years — the memory was still tormenting him.

'What happened then?' he asked.

'I collected my supplies and went home. I didn't go back into Redwood for maybe a month or two and by then the sheriff had given up on finding the man who had shot the bounty hunter.

'While I was in town the sheriff took me into his office and told me that my father had been killed trying to rob a bank in Wichita. I can't say I was heartbroke, Ben, and when I got home and told my ma it was as though she had been expecting it.

'We stayed on the farm for a couple more years and then my mother decided it was time to sell up — one of the neighbours had been pestering her to let him buy her out. There was nothing to keep her there except me and I was all for moving on. So she sold up and went to live with my sister Alice and her husband and baby, who had moved out to Taylorsville in Utah.

'Seems my sister and her husband had found religion and joined them Mormon folk out near Salt Lake City. They eventually moved back into Kansas and they now live up near Junction City.

'Anyways, after my mother decided to join them I stayed on for a few weeks to help the new owner and then, with dollars in my pocket from the sale, I headed out and finished up here in Progress.'

He paused as if wondering how to go on. Then he slumped forward in his seat.

'It was so long ago, Ben, I thought I had left it all behind, that nobody would know.' His voice was barely above a whisper. 'But somebody did. I don't know how he found out but Sam Duncan told me he knew.' Lane paused again and then added: 'He told me how bad it would look for me if I ever wanted to be town marshal and it got out I'd killed a man by shooting him in the back. And how would it go down with Lucy? Would she want to be married to a killer? He said he would keep my secret out of his newspaper if . . . '

'If you helped him pay for his gambling and his drinking.' Ben finished the sentence.

The young deputy nodded and Ben walked out of the cell. He hated the idea but he had just discovered a reason for Lane Cutler to want Sam Duncan dead.

6

Ben McCabe knew he had no choice but to keep his deputy in a cell. The evidence against him was mounting at every turn and even Ben's faith was beginning to weaken. He recalled the day, before he became town marshal of Progress, when he had saved Tommy Kane from the hangman. But was this the same? Was he as sure that Lane was innocent?

One person who had no doubts was waiting for him when he arrived at the Little Lady diner for his midday meal. Lucy Blake, young, petite and pretty, had been crying. Her eyes were red against her pale skin and long fair hair and she was being comforted by Carla Jack.

'Hello, Marshal McCabe.' It was a weak, unsmiling greeting from the young woman who was soon to marry

Lane. Ben felt uneasy. What could he say to the girl? He was grateful that Mrs Jack was there to offer some comfort.

'Lucy,' he said softly, removing his hat and sliding into a chair at his favourite table. 'I don't want you to worry — '

'But you've got Lane locked up,' she interrupted. 'Why shouldn't I worry? He couldn't do what they are saying. He couldn't kill Mr Duncan.'

Ben looked at Carla for support but he found none.

'I've got to do that, Lucy, until I sort this thing out. I don't think Lane killed him either, but it's the law. It's my job to find out who did it and, well, I guess that's going to take a bit of time.'

But there was nothing he could say to placate her and he decided against a meal. He had lost his appetite.

It was time to ask Lane a few more questions, like where he was when he was jumped by the Mexican and the tall man he called Vince. But once again Luther Bush stepped in to interrupt his plans.

Struggling for breath, the overweight

mayor of Progress tried to explain what had happened on his way to the marshal's office.

'I was coming to see you, Marshal, just to ask how your investigations were progressing and to offer any help if you needed it — you know we all believe in Lane — when he suddenly burst out of your office, knocked me clean off my feet and ran off into the street.'

He paused to dust down his suit, as if to emphasize his distress.

'I shouted at him to stop but he paid me no heed. Instead he just unhitched the nearest horse from the rail outside the saloon and rode off out of town, heading west at a gallop.'

Lane was on the run.

'It doesn't look good, Ben, does it? I mean, why did he run out when he knows the whole town's on his side?'

'I see what you're saying, Mayor, but right now I'm more interested in getting him back. Looks like I'll have to leave law and order to you until I do that. I've got a fugitive to catch.'

It was late afternoon and he was allowing his horse a slow walk after some hard riding when Ben suddenly found himself stopping in his tracks on the orders of a voice coming from behind a bush.

'I knew you'd come, Ben, but I wish you hadn't.'

Lane Cutler stepped out from his hiding-place, his rifle pointed at the marshal's chest. He took a few steps forward. Ben lowered the horse's reins and tipped his hat away from his face.

'So. You did kill Sam Duncan to keep him quiet? Is that what this means?'

'Everybody thinks I did, which makes it the same thing as I see it. Especially when they ever get round to choosing a jury.'

'Not everybody,' Ben said.

'How about you?'

'Me? I'm not so sure. Not after this.'

'Then who?'

'Lucy Blake for one.'

Lane lowered his rifle but kept a firm

grip on it. Lucy, the woman he was due to marry, still believed in him. And now he was running out on her.

'You've got to come back,' McCabe said. 'Leastways, I make it you've got two choices. Either I put you under arrest and you ride back to Progress with me or . . . '

'Or what?'

'Or you use that rifle.'

He waited before adding: 'The way I see it is that that mare there isn't yours, which makes you a horse thief. If you kill me there'll be others to come after you. And you can forget all about Lucy.'

'They can only hang me once,' the young deputy said sourly.

'And they'll only hang you if you killed Sam — or you kill me.'

He detected that Lane's resolve was weakening and he turned away and moved to remount his horse. 'So what's it to be, Lane? You going to shoot me, let me ride out or come back to town?'

He swung his horse round and headed back towards the road.

He had only gone a few yards when the call came.

'Hold it, Ben!'

McCabe pulled his horse to a halt, turned in the saddle and watched as Lane Cutler slid his rifle into the sheath in his saddle and climbed up on to the horse he had taken from outside the saloon a few hours earlier.

The marshal waited until the young deputy came alongside.

'I'm counting on you, Ben. I'm gambling with my life coming back with you.'

McCabe reached out and gripped the young man's shoulder.

'I know that, son. But I saw Lucy before I came looking for you. She believes in you, so I reckon that should be fine enough for me.'

He released his hold on the young man's shoulder. 'Tell me one thing. How did you get out of the cell?'

Lane smiled for the first time in many a day.

'You ought to be more careful where you leave the extra keys, Marshal.'

7

Mayor Luther Bush edged his way past the small group of town councillors and headed for the table at the far end of the hall that served as a church and meeting-place. He nodded politely to friends Slim Brennan, owner of the town's general store, rancher George Benson and Carson Grant, who owned the Grant Bank of Progress.

The room fell silent when Luther ordered his fellow councillors to take their seats and he slid into his place at the head of the table. He coughed, more as a token of his intention to get the meeting under way than as an attempt to clear his throat. He then banged on the table to open proceedings.

There was only one item on the agenda for this special meeting of the Progress town council.

'Gentlemen, we are here today to discuss what happened this morning when I tried to visit the marshal's office only to be knocked down in the street by our deputy marshal Lane Cutler.

'Now you all know how I feel about young Lane and this ridiculous accusation that he was the one who killed our friend Sam Duncan — and I am sure you all feel the same. The marshal is out there looking for him and hoping to persuade him to come back to town. But, after what happened today: young Lane breaking out of his cell and running off — even stealing a horse to make his getaway — I am beginning to ask myself, did he really kill Sam?'

There was a murmur of disagreement among the rest of the council, a few shakes of the head and a 'certainly not' from George Benson, but the mayor held up his hand for silence.

'I know — we don't want to believe it. But, well, Lane did run out and he did shout at me as he ran past. Now, it is not something I have told our marshal because I have respect for him and he has every faith in young Lane.'

'What was it, Luther? What did Lane say to you?'

The mayor put on a show of reluctance to continue. Eventually he said: 'Lane was cursing like a crazy man. Now I don't know if he really meant what he was saying but it sounded to me like . . . gentlemen, I would not wish this to reach some of the unsavoury types we have in Progress. Any word of this in the saloons and, well, there are some degenerate characters in town and who knows how they would react, given a few too many beers or a bad hand at the poker table — '

'What is it, Luther?' Brennan shouted, jumping to his feet.

Luther Bush let his gaze roam around the faces in front of him. Was this the time to tell them? What would happen if the word got out? He decided the time was right.

'He didn't stop to apologize for knocking me over,' he said, trying to lighten the mood.

'What did he say, Luther?' There was anger in the question.

'He said . . . 'I don't know why I've been locked up — Sam Duncan deserved to die.''

There were gasps of astonishment and snorts of disapproval from around the room.

But Luther Bush held up his hands for quiet. 'Please, gentlemen, like I've said, let us not be too determined to jump to the wrong conclusion. Lane is a young man and young men, as we all remember, do and say strange things. We mustn't be hasty in condemning him for words, however cruel.'

He examined the faces of the men in the room. They were not convinced.

'Gentlemen, the reason I called this meeting was to confirm our support for Marshal McCabe and I hope I have got your approval in telling him that, whatever the outcome of this unsavoury incident, he has our full support.'

The councillors nodded almost in

unison. Ben McCabe was their town marshal — in their view.

'But I must repeat,' the mayor concluded, 'what has been said in this room must go no further.'

They all agreed, but Luther knew that the Slim Brennan who was the town councillor and discreet general store owner was not the same Slim Brennan who spent long hours in the bar of the Silver Spur saloon.

The meeting broke up and the council members returned to their business — at exactly the same time that Ben McCabe was leading Lane Cutler back to his place behind bars.

*   *   *

Two days after Lane's return to the town jail Ben McCabe got his first hint that the mood in Progress was taking a sinister turn.

The marshal was winding down a busy day in the Silver Spur when a quiet poker game suddenly flared into a heated exchange of raised voices.

'Well, I'm tellin' you I ain't so sure. Yeah, he's a young kid and he's learnin' to be a peace officer, but that don't mean much from where I'm sittin'. Not from what I've been hearin' anyways.'

Jed Lennon was not known for his even temper or friendly personality and he was enjoying his moment.

The man directly across from him, Dan Sturk, threw a bill on to the pile in the middle of the table and grunted. He had known Lennon since they worked together on the railroad and had long since learned to steer clear of any arguments involving the older man when he was in one of his aggressive moods. Now was one of those times but Sturk did not get away so easily. Maddox, one of the other card-players, enjoyed riling Lennon.

'So what is it you've been hearing about young Cutler, then, Jed?'

Lennon studied his cards and then tossed a fistful of coins into the pile.

'I hear tell the young feller ain't all

he's said to be. I hear that he owed Sam Duncan and Sam was wanting to collect. 'Cept that young Cutler didn't want to pay.'

Dan Sturk snorted. He couldn't help himself. 'What's that supposed to mean?'

'It means that young Lane could have had a reason for killin' Sam. Hell, it's all over town that his badge was found in Sam Duncan's hand after the fire. And didn't he go missing after the killing?'

'But he's back now, ain't he?' Maddox protested. 'All locked up waiting for the circuit judge.'

'Sure he's back. But for how long? The judge maybe won't be here for another week and by then young Cutler could be out of the territory. And I'm saying something else. Next time the marshal won't do much to chase after him. I reckon McCabe knows that young Cutler's as guilty as hell and he isn't going to let him swing.'

Dan Sturk could resist no longer. 'That's horse shit, Jed. You haven't got any call to accuse Ben McCabe of anything like that. He's a good lawman.'

'Is he?'

Lennon's barked question caught Ben's attention. From his position at the end of the bar, where he had gone unnoticed by the card-players, he had listened with only passing interest. Now he waited to see how the latest twist in the argument would develop.

'Not what I heard!' Lennon snapped.

'You been hearing more strange voices, Jed?' Maddox chuckled. 'Must be that rotgut whiskey you drink.'

'I'm telling you all,' Lennon went on, undeterred, 'before he came to Progress McCabe was a deputy US marshal who gunned down a man in cold blood. Just out of sheer hate — nothing else — but the law didn't touch him. Even though they knew. Like I said, the law ain't no different to the rest of us — they stick together.'

Ben emptied his glass, left his place at the corner of the bar and strode across to the card table.

'Go on, Jed. I'd like to hear this.' Lennon stiffened as Ben towered over his left shoulder. 'Who am I supposed to have gunned down in cold blood, as you say?'

Lennon turned. 'Just what I've been hearing, Marshal. Maybe you had reasons. Maybe — '

'Forget the maybes, Jed, just tell me — tell us all — what it is you've been hearing.'

'Well, it was a long whiles ago, but I hear the guy's name was Jay Munroe, a ranch hand who crossed you once. The story is you waited and waited until you got him alone out on some open prairie in Arizona and you shot him and then you dumped his body in Rico for the townsfolk there to bury. Now tell us that ain't true.'

Ben was aware of four pairs of eyes staring up at him. There was a stunned silence before Dan Sturk posed the question.

'Is it true, Marshal? Did you kill this man Munroe?'

'It's true,' Ben said at last. 'It's not quite how Jed here tells it, but yes. I killed him. Out on the prairie near Rico. No witnesses.'

Ben turned and left the saloon. How had Jed Lennon learned about the killing of murderer, bank robber and the man who left him for dead in a Wyoming creek, Jay Munroe? As far as he was aware only two people in Progress knew about what happened in Arizona five years ago. One was Sam Duncan — and he was dead.

The other was a man he had trusted with the information before taking on the job of town marshal. Mayor Luther Bush.

★　★　★

Ben did not return to the hotel that night. Instead he thought he might be needed at the jailhouse. Jed Lennon was in the mood to start trouble and after a few more drinks he would more than likely to be able to stir up a few drunken cowhands to come calling. Ben did not anticipate anything approaching a lynch mob. Lane Cutler still had enough friends in town to see that didn't happen, but a drunken Jed Lennon could still be a handful. The lawman chuckled to himself at the idea of dumping Lennon into the vacant cell next to the one occupied by Lane.

The discovery that Lennon — and that meant anybody else who would listen — knew of his killing of Jay Munroe in circumstances that he had never been asked to explain worried Ben. It had happened. He could hardly deny that, but it had all been in the course of his duty as deputy US marshal. And it had also been personal. It was Munroe who had left him for dead with a bullet in his chest and another buried somewhere in the undergrowth after it had skimmed off his temple. To this day he still had the scar as a reminder of how close he had come to death and how the Kane family had saved his life. Five years after Munroe had shot him, when Ben was trying to prove young Tommy Kane innocent of a murder, he ran into Munroe again, selling whiskey and guns to renegade Indians. Ben knew that he had done Arizona and all points west a service when he killed Munroe, but if Lennon's twisted version of the truth ever grew in strength among the townsfolk of Progress his days as marshal would be over. And even his own choice of buying up George Benson's spread would no longer be an option. He would be run out of the territory.

Meanwhile Ben had questions of his own that needed answers. Who was the Mexican lying in an unmarked grave in the town cemetery? And who was the lank-haired Vince, who had beaten Lane senseless and, if the young lawman's story was accurate, had put two bullets in the Mexican? Where was this cabin where Lane had been held prisoner — and who was the mysterious city gent who had clearly been the boss?

Ben was still mulling over all these questions when he eventually slipped quietly into the vacant cell and settled down for a few hours' sleep. He had a peaceful night, undisturbed by any visit from Jed Lennon.

Lane was awake, pacing his cell when Ben eventually roused himself the following morning, but he was not in a talkative mood. Apart from an occasional grunt or monosyllabic response to the most innocent question or observation he made no attempt to communicate and, after serving him coffee and eggs, Ben left him to his own company. He had other things to do that morning and a meeting with the mayor of Progress was top of the list.

* * *

Luther Bush was angry. 'You told me that in confidence, Ben, and I respected that. You're looking in the wrong place if you want to find out who would tell somebody like Jed Lennon something you'd rather keep to yourself — something that could have you marked down as a cold-blooded killer. I resent the idea that you would think I would betray you.'

Ben slumped into an armchair, suitably chastened.

'Sorry, Mayor, but only you and Sam Duncan knew about what happened outside of Rico five years ago, and Sam's dead.'

'And dead men don't talk. Is that it, Ben?'

'Not what I was thinking, but from what I've learned these past few days Sam was the sort of man who liked to keep his secrets.'

'You'll have to explain that, Marshal.'

Ben rubbed his chin. What he had just said suddenly hit home. Sam Duncan was quite happy to extort money by threatening to use his newspaper to expose people who had secrets they wanted to stay that way. Yet he knew about Ben and the Munroe killing but had made no approach for money to keep his silence. 'Someday, Mayor, someday.'

'Well, it sure wasn't me, and if you

say Sam was the only other person in Progress who knew the truth then there's your answer. I hate to say it about a dead friend but I can't think of any other way Lennon got to find out.' He paused and stared at Ben before adding: 'But tell me something. Why are you so keen to keep it a secret? From what you told me you were only doing your job. You were a deputy US marshal and this man — this Munroe — was selling guns to renegades. You said that he was also a murderer. From where I stand you had every right to kill him.'

'Maybe you're right, Mayor, but when I came to Progress it was to get away from my past, from people like Munroe. He would have friends, others I came across who . . . well, let's say I wouldn't invite them into my town. And Progress is now my town. You and the people here don't need visits from hard-nosed gunslingers who fancy their chances of outshooting the man who killed Jay Munroe. This is a nice, quiet town. No drifters, not too many

Saturday drunks — just good, law-abiding folk who want a quiet life.'

Luther Bush smiled. 'And much of that is down to you, Ben. Sam's death has stunned everybody in town, and to think that it might be your own deputy who did the killing . . . well, that's bad.'

'Hold it, Mayor. I reckon Lane might be a victim here. His story may take a bit of believing but I'm starting to think that he could be telling the truth. It's hard to ignore a dead Mexican and all those bruises.'

'But why, Marshal? Why would somebody — we don't know who or where they came from — why would they want to fix a young feller like Lane Cutler for a fire and a murder? It makes no sense.'

Ben lifted his hat off the back of the chair and put it on in readiness to leave.

'I can't argue with that. It makes no sense. But I'm sure it will. I am going to find out who burned down the newspaper office in an attempt to cover up the killing of Sam Duncan and left evidence to involve Lane. But my guess is that young Lane had nothing to do with it.'

'I wish you well, Ben, but you're running out of time. The circuit judge will be here in a few days. I'd be interested to know how you're going to clear Lane's name.'

'I am going to find out where the name Quillan fits in.'

They shook hands and Luther stood in his doorway to watch Ben McCabe stride off towards the Little Lady dining rooms. He waited until the marshal had gone into the café before turning and going back into his house.

He didn't delay. Grabbing his hat, he hurried out of the back of the house, saddled his horse — this was no time for a leisurely buggy ride — and headed out of town.

He had important business to discuss away from the prying eyes and ears of the people of Progress.

* * *

The early afternoon was hot and stifling and Luther felt the sweat dripping down his neck and inside his shirt. He stopped his horse, mopped his brow and studied the long track that led to the impressive ranch house.

He had been in the saddle for more than four hours but even after such a tiring ride he was still uncertain of his next move.

The man he had come to see was unlikely to take kindly to what Luther had to say. Maybe he would eventually agree that the whole scheme had been madness from the start and that a bullet was the quickest and best way to solve all their problems.

Only now did he realize that Joe Quillan's quest for vengeance had brought him more trouble than he needed. The death of Sam Duncan had meant his problems were over — but Quillan had to have his extra pound of flesh.

Luther was sure his partner would not take kindly to the news that 'Quillan' had been the last word from a drunken man two days before he was murdered, and that Marshal Ben McCabe knew that. It was information that Luther would have to use to protect himself and leave Quillan to do what he would be good at — ordering the death of a troublesome lawman.

He mopped his brow again, nudged his horse forward and headed through the wide gate with the ostentatious lettering that announced he was entering the Bar-Q Ranch.

The wide open spaces leading up to the big house ensured that any unwelcome visitors would never have the chance to catch the owner unawares.

So it was no surprise to Luther Bush to learn that he had been spotted while he was still almost half a mile away, or that the ranch owner was waiting on the veranda to meet him. There was no welcoming smile, no offer of a handshake; the man with the neatly trimmed grey beard simply waved his pearl-handled walking-stick towards the door and limped into the house behind his visitor.

8

Lane Cutler stirred in his cell, suddenly wakened and aware of a shuffling noise outside the barred window of the jail. Sliding off his bed, Lane checked that Ben McCabe was still in a deep sleep in the far corner of his office before climbing back on to the bunk and stretching up to peer out into the darkness.

'Who's out there?' His voice was no more than a whisper but even as he spoke he feared that he might wake the sleeping marshal.

'Lane! You've got to get out of there.' The answering voice also came back at a whisper. A female whisper.

'Lucy? What the hell — '

'Please, Lane. There's no time. You've got to get out. Pa's just had a visit from the mayor. Mr Bush is worried that there's talk of a lynch mob in town. Jed

Lennon and some of his friends in the Silver Spur.'

Lane relaxed.

'Go home, Lucy. They talked about that last night. Ben knew all about it and they didn't come. Jed Lennon's just a big talker. He won't do nothing.'

'No, Lane, you don't understand. This was tonight.'

'Tonight? You sure?'

'The mayor told Pa he heard it himself. He tried to calm them all down but . . . Lane, you gotta get out.'

The young prisoner thought for a moment. Ben McCabe had talked him into giving himself up, he had promised him he would get a fair trial, he had told him nothing would happen to him if he was innocent. And Ben was not only his boss. He was his friend.

'Go home, Lucy,' he said at last. 'I'll wake the marshal. He'll know what to do.'

'But, Lane — '

'Go home!' he almost barked the order and it was loud enough to stir

Ben from his sleep. Lane dropped to the floor and strode across the cell to face the stirring marshal.

'Ben — we got trouble coming.'

He related the story he had just been told by Lucy and watched in anticipation as Ben strapped on his gunbelt. Then the marshal retrieved the keys from the desk drawer and unlocked the cell.

'I reckon Lucy's right, Lane. There's only one way to stop any shooting and that's for you not to be here when Lennon and his crowd arrive looking for your neck. I know you didn't kill Sam.'

'You know? How?'

'No time for that now,' Ben said, pulling open the cell door. 'I'm trusting you. There's a small barn on the edge of George Benson's place. I want you to go there for tonight. I can handle Lennon. I might even need your cell to keep him quiet for the rest of the night,' he added with a smile. 'But the judge will be in town day after tomorrow. It'll soon be over, Lane.'

Lane Cutler's face showed that he was far from convinced that the pending arrival of the circuit judge was in his favour but he said: 'Thanks, Ben. I won't let you down.'

Ben suddenly moved forward and gripped his young deputy in a bear hug.

'I'm counting on that, son.'

He released Lane and pushed him towards the back door of the office.

'You ought to be on your way. There's no telling how long it will be before Lennon and his gang of rope-crazy drunks get here.'

He stood at the back door of the jailhouse, watched his young deputy ride out into the night, then returned to his office chair to wait for the arrival of Lennon's gang.

But the marshal of Progress spent the night alone. No lynch mob came.

9

The sun, low in the eastern sky, was a deep-red glow which almost blinded Ben McCabe as he approached the gate leading to the Benson spread that was to become his own.

That day could not come soon enough. He had long since decided that his life as a lawman — even in the quiet backwater that was Progress County — was as good as over.

The fire, the murder of newspaperman Sam Duncan, whose position as an upright citizen was now coming under a cloud of rumour, and the arrest of a young man he believed to be innocent had only hastened McCabe's desire to hang up his guns and his badge and settle down to life as a small-ranch owner . . . and maybe even find time to devote to the one missing link in his life, a woman to share his remaining years.

McCabe had little knowledge of ranching; ever since his schooldays he had taken an interest in the law and his only experience of cattle had come during the war, when he found himself driving steers across the prairies to feed the Union troops.

The Benson place was more than big enough for his needs — he had no intention of challenging the cattle barons of the county — and with the present foreman keen to stay on alongside his son, he knew he would not lack expert help when the time came.

He paused to run a bandanna across his brow. Although it was still early the rising sun was already threatening another baking hot day and McCabe would be happy when he retrieved his prisoner, returned him to the jail and he could wait for the arrival of the circuit judge.

His thoughts were still on the few days ahead when he spotted the horse. Grazing lazily beyond a clump of bushes, it was the bay that Lane Cutler had used to ride out of town the previous night. Puzzled at the sight of the riderless horse, McCabe dismounted and strolled across to the clearing in the brush.

He had taken only a few strides when he witnessed the sight that was to destroy his plans and to change his future.

Lane Cutler was hanging from a large oak tree.

* * *

Ben McCabe cradled the lifeless body of his young deputy and Lane's words came rushing back to haunt him.

I'm gambling with my life, coming back with you.

Ben whispered for the third time: 'I'm sorry, son. I let you down. I should have kept you in the cell and stood up against Jed Lennon. I'm so sorry.'

Slowly, he got to his feet and lifted Cutler's body into the saddle, remounted his own horse and headed back to Progress. It was a slow, desolate journey and the time was consumed by McCabe's increasing belief that the man who had hanged

111

the young deputy could be found in the Silver Spur saloon.

The hours that followed his discovery of the body only served to strengthen the lawman's conviction that he had failed the young man now lying in the funeral parlour in Progress's main street. The only thought that occupied his worried mind was how Jed Lennon and his sidekicks had known that Lane was being temporarily transferred from the jailhouse.

Could there be any doubt that Lennon and his band of drunkards had carried out their threat and turned into a lynch mob? With each passing minute McCabe felt the urge for vengeance growing ever stronger.

I'm gambling with my life, coming back with you.

It was a gamble that had cost him his life. The law had failed Lane Cutler and in Progress County Ben McCabe was the law.

Breaking the news to Lucy Blake was another torturous duty. He thought he had seen all the grief the world could offer during his long career as a law officer but when Lucy broke down in tears, those years of experience failed him.

'Why?' she pleaded through her heart-wrenching sobs. 'Why did you move him? Tell me why?'

How could he tell her he did it because he thought it would be safer? That her young man had been hanged by the lynch mob he had been expecting but who never arrived at the jailhouse. Instead they somehow learned that the man they wanted had been moved to a secret hideaway.

Leaving Lucy to be comforted by her mother, McCabe returned to his office. His firm belief was that Lennon was the main man behind the lynching; the threats reported by Mayor Luther Bush were more than enough for Ben to arrest the one-time railroad worker even though he knew that the increasing rage and thirst for vengeance were sure to cloud his judgement. He needed to make a decision. The longer he delayed the easier it would be for Lennon to connive an alibi. He had enough associates who shared his views to vouch for the fact that he never left their sight all night, drinking in the Silver Spur until he was too drunk to stand let alone organize a lynch party.

Ben poured himself a mug of cold coffee and slumped into his chair. Across the room the empty cell was a painful reminder that it should still be occupied by a promising young deputy wrongly accused of murder. Slamming his mug on to the desk, Ben came to a sudden decision. He would call on Luther Bush and —

Before he could move, the office door burst open. The marshal had a visitor. Jed Lennon stood in the doorway.

10

When he spoke Lennon's voice was little more than a feeble croak, but it was not the sound that shocked Ben — he had heard too many heavy drinkers of cheap whiskey sound exactly the same — it was the man's appearance. His face was battered and bruised, his left eye almost completely closed by a large swelling above his jaw and his right arm was strapped in a makeshift sling.

'I hear you're looking for me, Marshal,' he rasped. It clearly caused him serious pain to speak but McCabe was short on sympathy for the man he believed was responsible for the death of his young deputy. If not by his own hand then he was certainly the ringleader of any lynch mob.

'That's right, Lennon. Looks like you and somebody else have saved me a lot of trouble.'

His visitor ignored the lawman's jibe and slumped into the nearest chair.

'You reckon I had something to do with young Cutler's death?'

'Did you?'

'Listen, Marshal. I don't know what you've been hearing or what somebody has been saying about me. Sure, I said some things about that kid and I sure as hell ain't crying that he's dead. Far as I can see he got what he deserved for killing Sam Duncan, but I didn't do it. How could I? You only gotta look at me.'

'So tell me, Lennon. What happened?'

Jed Lennon shuffled in his seat and rested his arm on the desk.

'I'm here to put you straight, Marshal. I heard what Mayor Bush has been saying about me and, sure, maybe it's true . . . at least some of it. I was shooting my mouth off in the Silver Spur last night. But that's all it was. Drinkin' talk.'

'You do a lot of that, Lennon,' Ben put in.

'Ain't that the case?' the injured man

agreed. 'And it got me into a whole lot of trouble last night.'

'So tell me about it.'

Lennon rubbed his jaw and tried to force a smile. It didn't happen.

'Look, McCabe, you've known me a long time. You've even locked me up in that cell over there a few times. I ain't no killer.' He paused, rubbed his injured arm and continued: 'There was this kid — seems he was a good friend of Cutler. He didn't like what I was saying . . . '

'What were you saying, Lennon?'

'I reckoned that Cutler should be strung up and if the law wouldn't do it then we should.'

'Who's we?'

'The people of Progress. Sam Duncan was a good friend of ours. We didn't want to see his killer walk away because some smart city lawyer sweet-talked a judge and jury out of it.

'This kid told me to shut my mouth and when I told him to butt out he turned real nasty. There was a ruckus and the next thing I know this kid's all het up and scrambling over the table to get at me.

'He went crazy. Kicking and punching. Caught me by surprise, though maybe if I'd been a few years younger I could have . . . ' His voice tailed away.

'Who was this kid?'

Ben was still not convinced that Lennon was telling him the whole truth, even with the evidence of a badly bruised face and a damaged arm.

'He reckoned he was a ranch hand from up north. A real hothead. It took old Doc Miller a couple of hours to patch me up.'

Lennon struggled to his feet. 'Like I said, Marshal, you're gonna have to look somewhere else for the man who lynched Cutler, though I don't know why you'd want to find him. An eye for an eye . . . ain't that what the Good Book says?'

What Jed Lennon would know about the Good Book Ben could not start to guess but when his visitor shuffled out back into the street he slumped into his chair.

If Lennon was telling the truth in saying that he had spent most of the night being patched up by Doc Miller then it was a sure thing that he had not been part of the lynch mob. His story would be easy enough to check; Jonas Miller was an honest man whom Ben knew he could trust.

But if the killer wasn't Lennon — and the evidence of his innocence was growing — then who had wanted to see Lane Cutler dead? And why a lynching? Ben would have thought that a bullet in the back in a dark alley one night would have been just as effective.

The more he thought about it, the more he wondered what exactly was behind the killing.

According to Lane he had been held prisoner in a barn for three days, during which time he had repeatedly been seen in town by Sam Duncan's wife. But if Ben believed his young deputy Mrs Duncan must have been mistaken. So what had she seen? Somebody dressed in Lane's clothes? Somebody Sam had agreed to meet at the newspaper office that night?

That would explain the discovery of the deputy's badge that the dead newspaperman had been clutching . . . evidence that Lane Cutler had been in the newspaper office some time before the killing.

Whoever had planned and carried out the murder wanted Lane to pay for it. They wanted him to suffer. To face the hangman's noose. There was a serious desire for vengeance in the heart of whoever was Lane's killer.

And the more he thought about it the more he was led to the name Quillan.

McCabe poured himself another coffee as he puzzled over the dilemma. One thought that struck him was the notion that, like so many of the towns-folk of Progress, Lane had a secret, known only to Sam Duncan. If that was the case it had cost both men their lives and somebody out there had known about that secret.

Ben was sure of one thing: whoever

was behind the lynching wanted much more than to see Lane Cutler dead. They had gone to a lot of trouble to make sure that he was arrested and made to face the threat of the noose. Until . . . ?

Ben got to his feet with the sudden movement of a man hit by a startling thought.

The real killer, who had set out to have Lane arrested in the belief that the evidence was so strong that he would surely be found guilty, had developed doubts. He must have been coming to realize that he couldn't rely on a judge and jury to give him what he wanted.

Ben was still deep in thought, toying with his empty coffee mug, when he had another visitor. This time it was a young man, fair-haired with piercing blue eyes, broad shoulders and standing six feet tall. The only flaws on a clean-shaven, handsome face were a slight swelling of his jaw and an ugly scar above his left eye.

'What can I do for you, son?' Ben

tried to make the question as friendly as he could but he was in no mood for another caller.

'I came to see you, Marshal, because I think you could do with my help to find a killer.'

The lawman got up from his chair and studied the young man. He pointed to the swelling on the side of his face.

'Who gave you that?'

The stranger rubbed his face.

'I guess you might already know that, Marshal. The man who just left here a few minutes ago. I waited for him to go because ... well, you saw what happened to him the last time we met. He was drunk and he was shooting his mouth off about Lane Cutler, how he should be hanged and if the law wouldn't do it he sure as hell would.'

'Jed Lennon,' Ben told him. 'That's his name.'

'I didn't ask,' the young stranger said. 'But Lane Cutler was my best friend and I don't think he should have been locked up. He didn't kill anybody.'

'What's your name, kid?'

'Corey Hayes — and I ain't a kid. I'm the same age as Lane was.'

'Well, listen to me, Corey Hayes. I already feel bad enough about the killing of Lane Cutler and don't need some young hothead causing more trouble than I've already got. Lennon has a big mouth and a temper that gets him into trouble. But, much as I'd like to be wrong, I don't think he killed your friend. You made sure of that by sending him to Doc Miller's.'

Hayes shrugged.

'I guess I already knew that but he deserved what I gave him.'

Ben smiled. 'Yes, you're right about that and no mistake. You say you were a friend of Lane. How long had you known him?'

Hayes crouched on the edge of the office desk.

''Most all my life. We grew up together, neighbours and schoolfriends.'

Ben waited for him to continue.

'My father was sheriff in Redwood

when we were kids. Lane's old man ran out on them during the war and Lane spent a lot of time at our place. I owe him.'

'That may be, Hayes, but it's not my concern. Right now I've got enough trouble without a kid with a grievance turning vigilante.'

'Like I said, I am not a kid and I am not planning to be a vigilante, Marshal. I just want to help find whoever killed Lane. Whoever it was who strung Lane up deserves the same.'

Ben studied the young stranger more closely. Maybe he could be of some help. There was only so much that Ben could do alone; now that Lennon had been ruled out he did not have a single lead on the identity of the man behind the hanging, and there was no reason to doubt that Corey Hayes wished to bring his friend's killer to justice.

There was just one problem for the marshal. He had never seen Corey Hayes before: not around town, never in Lane's company; the young deputy had never even mentioned his name, so where had he come from?

'When did you last see Lane?' he asked.

Hayes replied without hesitation: 'Two — maybe three years back.' He saw McCabe's look of surprise and grinned. 'Looks like you want an explanation, Marshal. Like how I just happen to be in Progress the day after my friend ends up being killed by some lynch mob?'

Ben nodded. 'It might help me believe you.'

The young man reached inside his shirt pocket and pulled out a sheet of paper. He thrust it towards the marshal.

'This,' he said.

Ben unfolded the paper and read the message. He passed the sheet back to his visitor.

'You owe him?' Ben asked.

'Like the telegram says, Marshal, I owe him.'

'Tell me about it.'

Corey Hayes slid into a chair, threw

his hat on the desk and helped himself to a mug of coffee.

'Before he came to Progress Lane was just a young cowhand on my uncle's ranch. We were larking about, just like the old days when we were kids before the war. I got myself tangled up in some weeds in a fast-running stream that came after some heavy snow melted, and I would sure have drowned if Lane hadn't dragged me out. So when he wrote to me to say that he was in trouble over killing some newspaperman he hardly knew, then I thought I ought to come and see what I could do to help. Now it looks like I got here too late.'

Corey Hayes suddenly got to his feet. 'Maybe you won't let me help you, Marshal, but I don't aim to leave Progress until I find out what happened to my friend.'

'You sound like a gutsy kid, Corey — yeah, you are not a kid — but I think you should leave this to the law to sort out.'

'Sounds like you're warning me off, Marshal,' Hayes said huffily.

Ben McCabe thought about that. Maybe he was being a bit harsh on the kid, who only wanted to help hunt down his friend's killer. And perhaps he could be useful, somebody who knew Lane better than he did.

'Take a seat, Corey,' Ben said after a lengthy silence. 'I'll say this for you, son, I think I might be seeing something of myself in you so . . . let's talk about it.'

An hour later Corey Hayes was sworn in as a deputy town marshal and Ben McCabe knew he wasn't fighting a lone battle in his search for the killer of Lane Cutler. Even the help of a young man not yet twenty-two years of age was more than he had at the start of the day.

★ ★ ★

Luther Bush shouted angrily at his wife. His sour mood had not improved since his second meeting with Joe Quillan the day after Lane Cutler's lynching.

'I'll be back when I'm good and ready, woman!' he snapped, taking his hat from its rack behind the door and storming out of the house.

Life was getting tricky for the mayor of Progress and Quillan was not helping. The cattleman was becoming even more power crazy and was threatening to move his men into town on a regular basis. Luther would be able to handle the occasional Saturday night visit from a bunch of drunken cowhands — or at least Ben McCabe would; but if their visits were regular, then Progress would become just another lawless town, ignored by the state's hierarchy and putting paid to Bush's dreams of a seat in the legislature.

Wasn't that what he and Quillan had planned all along? But the meeting had gone badly.

'Now just you get this, Luther,' Quillan had snarled when Bush explained the reason for his visit. 'I didn't put you into Progress so you could come running here every time you felt like wetting your pants over something your marshal said. It seems to me I might have to send my men in there to sort out your Ben McCabe. Now that you've been stupid enough to throw him my name maybe it's time I took over that town good and proper. Vince would make a good marshal, don't you think?'

Joe Quillan had ruled Progress County with an iron fist, but from the distance of his extensive Bar-Q ranch. Luther Bush was a puppet mayor, bought and paid for by the Quillan family, so he needed all his persuasive powers to convince Joe that he should delay any move into town.

'I can handle McCabe, Joe. He trusts me. He don't know you, so giving him your name isn't going to help him. It's just that I have to think of a way of getting him to look somewhere else for whoever killed young Cutler. He's never gonna come here.'

'You told me you had that drunk Lennon marked up for McCabe.'

Luther's shoulders slumped.

'Some kid beat him up in the Silver

Spur. He spent the night with old Doc Miller while . . . ' His voice tailed off. He could not bring himself to utter the words forming in his mind.

Joe Quillan suddenly put his arm around the mayor's shoulder. His smile was neither warm nor genuine but Luther knew better than to move away.

'Here's what we do, old friend,' the cattleman said quietly. 'You have two days to convince your marshal that there is nothing to connect the Quillan name to Sam Duncan or the boy Cutler's killing. After that — well, Vince is getting restless, stuck out here away from the action, and now that the deputy's out of the way there's that pretty young thing Lucy Blake to think about.'

Luther had left the Bar-Q and headed straight for the saloon. He had drunk too much; he had found himself a whore to spend a few hours with before heading home and now, a day later, he still had to confront Ben McCabe with a story that would guide him away from the Quillans.

Why for Chris'sakes had that crazy Vince not let the law deal with Lane Cutler? Old man Quillan had already made sure that the circuit judge would have been bought and paid for and that the jury would do as they were ordered.

Lane Cutler had been a dead man walking. It would only have been a matter of time before Vince could watch the man he had vowed to kill swing from a rope legally.

Luther dismounted outside the Silver Spur. A few stiff drinks were what he needed to face Ben McCabe. Just then a familiar figure stepped out of the saloon into the harsh sunlight. It was a chance meeting that sent a chill down the spine of the mayor of Progress.

The appearance in town of the Bar-Q's foreman, Zak Hardin, meant that Quillan had decided not to give him the two days he had promised. Hardin could be in Progress for only one reason: to keep a watchful eye on him. And when Hardin was around, Vince Quillan and bloodshed were

131

never far away. It was the sight of the sour-faced figure in black that forced Luther into a sudden change of mind. As far as he was concerned, McCabe, Quillan and the rest could rot in hell.

It was time to get out of town, for it was Hardin who had gunned down Sam Duncan in the back and set the newspaper office ablaze. Even if it had been Luther who had placed the deputy badge in the dead newspaperman's hand to add strength to the evidence against Cutler he wanted no part in any more killings. Ducking behind his horse, he waited for Hardin to pass on down the street towards the small café. Luther then headed for the bank. It was time to take out his money, collect the gold he had hidden away in his office at the house and head south. Texas maybe. The quiet life in Progress was over. It was time to do what he had been thinking about since the fire. Sam had been his friend: at least, the nearest thing he had to a friend.

But fortune was not ready to smile

on the life of Luther Bush. Zak Hardin was not the only man he had to worry about. A newly appointed young deputy marshal was carrying out his instructions to the letter.

'I've got a feeling that our mayor knows a lot more than he's telling us,' Ben McCabe had explained when handing over the shiny new badge. 'I want you to keep a close watch on Mister Bush and tell me where he goes and who he sees.'

Corey Hayes nodded. 'And what will you be doing, Mr McCabe?'

Ben smiled. 'That will have to stay my business for now, Corey.'

* * *

George Benson shuffled across the room, poured a couple of drinks from a whiskey decanter and handed one to his visitor.

Benson had been born on the ranch that he now owned but was about to sell to Ben McCabe.

'Sixty-four years I've lived here,' he

said with a sigh. 'I reckon I have earned my time in the sun.'

'I think you have, George,' McCabe said, sipping his whiskey. 'And I can tell you I'll have the money for you inside the next few days. But you can stay on as long as you need.'

Benson laughed, a loud, full-throated guffaw.

'Ben, don't you think sixty-four years is long enough in one place? My daughter can't wait for me to move into her place and I can't wait either, so thanks for your offer but as soon as that bank draft comes through I will be on the next stage out of here.'

Ben emptied his glass and it was quickly refilled by the old man.

'But you didn't come out here to tell me something I already knew. I heard about your young deputy getting strung up out here on this ranch. Is that why you're here?'

Ben put down his glass.

'I'm looking for some information that might help. I have been town marshal in Progress for about three years — '

'Three and a half,' the old man interrupted. 'I was in town the day Luther Bush took you on.'

'Three and a half,' Ben conceded. 'I'm not going to argue with somebody who knows about these things. Since I came here I've got to know most folk in the county but until Sam Duncan was killed I never heard the name Quillan. Does it mean anything to you?'

Benson's smile had no trace of humour.

'Joe Quillan. No, it's not a name you'll hear much in Progress, even if he's just about the biggest cattle trader this side of the mountains. His Bar-Q ranch covers most of the county and then some, and if he had his way he'd be standing right here now.'

'He tried to buy this ranch?'

'Once or twice.' The old man chuckled. 'But he eventually got the message and backed off.' He paused before adding: 'Maybe it's because he reckons I'm family.'

Ben waited for the old man to continue but George took his time, refilling the glasses, circling the room as if deep in thought and then slumping into a large armchair.

'It was a long time ago,' he said with a heavy sigh. 'We were young cadets at West Point and, if I might admit to something, not the best officer material the place had ever seen. I think that if I had not been introduced to Alison Quillan at a local dance I might have gone down the same road as her brother. So at least I have him to thank for a wonderful wife and a marriage that lasted more than thirty years.'

Ben's puzzled frown prompted the old man to hurry on. 'Joe may be a rich and respected businessman these days but maybe nobody has ever taken a close look at how he started. We fought alongside each other against the Mexicans and in the Navajo wars down in New Mexico. Those battles gave him a taste for killing.

'Killing and power. And when he was through there he teamed up with a group of Texans who formed themselves into a gang of rustlers and bank robbers, plundering small towns and farms along the border. There was a price on their heads but Joe managed to shake off the law and turned up in these parts some twenty years ago with his young wife and two boys. When the war came Joe threw in his lot with the rebels but he got himself shot up in the Battle of Ball's Bluff. His war was over before it started. Next thing he is back here staking out a place some thirty miles out of town for him and his two sons.'

Benson paused and took another drink of his whiskey. He offered Ben a refill but the marshal placed his hand over the glass.

'What about Mrs Quillan?' Ben asked.

'She died young,' Benson said, then got to his feet. 'But all this happened long ago. Why all the interest in Quillan now?'

'I don't know, George. It's just a

name that came up.'

Benson got to his feet and strolled across the room to the open door leading to the veranda at the front of the house. Outside the sun was high in a clear sky, the wind was light. He leaned on the rail and was studying the greenery of his grazing pastures when the rifle bullet hit him full in the chest. His whiskey glass smashed against the veranda steps and the ranch owner fell backwards, crashing back into the room. Instantly another bullet ripped into the framework of the open door and a third hit the writhing man in the stomach.

Ben leapt from his chair and dashed across the room, gun at the ready. A quick glance was enough ... the rifleman was out of range and already mounted and making his getaway. The marshal turned and knelt beside the injured man, who was spluttering and coughing blood.

'Easy, George,' the marshal said in an effort to offer some comfort. But he did not need to be told . . . George Benson was dying. Struggling to gather his breath, he pulled Ben closer to him.

His words came in short gasps, the words of a dying man. But the marshal of Progress got the message.

The man he needed to talk to . . . the man who had arrived in Progress on the same stage as Joe Quillan all those years ago was Luther Bush.

★ ★ ★

Ben McCabe left Silas Jones's funeral parlour and headed straight for Luther Bush's house. He had delivered the body of George Benson to the town's undertaker and left instructions for the burial of the ranch owner before, grim-faced and angry, he set off to challenge the mayor for an explanation of the dying words of the murdered man.

What had George Benson been trying to tell him about the connection between Bush and Joe Quillan? And what had that friendship — if in fact there was anything between the two men — to do with the death of Lane Cutler or the killing of Sam Duncan?

And why had the mayor pretended that the name meant nothing to him?

It was the murder of the newspaperman that had been the start of the troubles for the marshal in the final few weeks before his retirement and the quiet life of a small ranch owner. It was clear now to Ben that Lane Cutler had had nothing to do with Duncan's death and that Duncan himself was not the upright citizen most of the town had believed him to be.

He was a man who knew too many secrets . . . secrets he threatened to reveal in the pages of the *Progress Leader* unless he was paid for his silence.

Lane Cutler had paid, but what did he have to hide? Whatever it was it had clearly cost him his life and unless Ben was badly mistaken the mayor was somehow connected. Bush may not have been directly involved in the lynching but it was the lawman's guess that he knew

140

more than he was saying.

The Bush house was well back from the rest of the residences at the north end of town, standing alone in its own grounds of well-kept greenery and flower-beds. It was a large, two-storey building at the end of a long pathway. A grey mare grazed in a small paddock alongside an abandoned buggy. But there was no sign of Luther's pride and joy, a black stallion.

Ben climbed the three steps leading up to the house and was about to knock on the door when he realized that it was slightly open. He pushed it further and called out the mayor's name.

There was no reply.

'Luther!' he repeated. 'It's Marshal McCabe. We have to talk.'

Again there was no answer. Instead, Ben could hear a sobbing sound coming from the room across the hallway to his right.

'Mayor!' he tried again. This time, when he still got no answer he entered the hallway cautiously but fully alert.

The sobbing from the nearby room grew louder.

McCabe pushed open the door to discover Martha Bush on her knees, rocking backwards and forwards, her arms wrapped around her husband. Blood covered the front of her dress and Ben did not need a second look to realize that Luther Bush was dead.

She did not look up when Ben entered the room. She did not even know he was there.

He crouched down beside her, putting his arm around her shoulder in an attempt to offer comfort. She turned her head, looked directly into his eyes, but there was no sign that she even recognized him.

'He's dead,' she sobbed softly. 'They just came in and killed him. Luther's dead.'

She turned away and continued to rock slowly, cradling her dead husband's head.

Ben got to his feet and studied the room. The scene was one of chaos. Furniture was smashed and scattered everywhere. A table and chairs had been overturned and a flower vase and a mirror lay shattered on the carpet.

He returned his attention to the mayor's wife. Slowly and gently he released the dead man from her grip and led her to an armchair.

'He's dead,' she repeated. 'They just came in and killed him.'

Ben took this as his chance.

'Who came, Mrs Bush? Who killed your husband?'

She didn't answer at first, just staring into space. Eventually, she regained her voice but it was little more than a whisper.

'Two men came in. They . . . argued and they fought and then . . . and then they . . . they shot my Luther. They shot him dead.'

The sobbing intensified but Ben had to press on.

'Who were they, Mrs Bush? Did they say anything?'

Martha Bush looked at him through tear-filled eyes.

'Say anything? They . . . they wanted to know about the money. The money and the gold. They talked about gold.' Ben waited. 'One of them hit my husband with his rifle butt and knocked him down.'

Slowly and painfully, Martha Bush described what had happened. Two men she had never seen before suddenly burst into the house as Luther was preparing to leave for what he said was a conference of town dignitaries in Wichita and he would be gone for a few days.

Although Martha had never seen the men before she thought that her husband knew at least one of them, perhaps both. They argued and fought and the two men started smashing up the furniture.

One of the intruders — Martha remembered he was a tall, thin man with shoulder-length hair — started breaking up the place and when Luther tried to stop him he shot Luther in the chest. Ben was about to leave when the woman, who had managed to bring her sobbing under control, suddenly grabbed his arm.

'There was one thing I remember,' she said quietly. 'Luther asked the tall one a question — I didn't hear what it was but I heard what the man said. He laughed in Luther's face and said: 'Of course he knows, you fool! It was Joe who sent us.'

★ ★ ★

An hour's ride outside Progress three men pulled their horses to a halt and dismounted. Zak, Vince and Jake Lucas needed their rest. Together they led their horses to the stream, quenched their own thirsts and crouched in the shade to escape from the stifling heat of the sun.

Hardin was the first to speak. 'You're sure you finished off that man Benson?'

It sounded like an accusation and Vince scowled at the question aimed at him.

'You want to go back and check?' he snapped. 'I hit him full in the chest. He went down and he didn't get back up. Like I said, he had a visitor. Couldn't see who it was but, yeah, I got the old man.'

'This visitor? He didn't get a look at you?'

It was Vince's turn to smirk. 'He fired a couple of shots but they wouldn't have hit a barn. I was out of there before he could figure out where the bullets had come from.

'Anyways, I got my man. How did you two settle with Bush?'

Hardin lit himself a cheroot.

'You see his horse over there, don't you? Seemed kinda stupid to leave it standing there just grazing and doin' nothing seeing as how the old mayor won't be needing it any more. Besides, Jake and me needed it to carry the money and the gold he was planning to run off with.' He chuckled but there was no humour in it.

'We felt sorry for his old lady.

146

Couldn't shut her up from crying so we just left her sobbing over her dead man.'

Vince stared coldly at the foreman.

'You just walked out and left her! Are you crazy? Soon as you walk into town she'll remember you.'

Hardin blew smoke into Vince's face.

'She was so scared she wouldn't recognize her own mother. Outside of that, Joe said nothing about killing Luther's wife. Just shut him up and bring the gold. Those were his orders.'

'That's right, Vince, Joe said nothing about killing a woman,' said Jake Lucas, speaking for the first time.

Vince turned away in disgust. He knew that the hired help were not let in on the reasons for the killings and he was not going to tell them. They were paid well enough to do as they were told without asking questions.

But there were at least two loose ends: the stranger at the Benson place and Mrs Bush.

He was fairly sure that the stranger

hadn't spotted him but he did not feel the same about the Bush woman's memory for faces. Jake's red hair and freckled complexion weren't easy to forget and Hardin was an ugly bastard in anybody's eyes. The old man wasn't going to like the news. The whole plan had been to cut off any notions of a connection between the Quillans and the killings of Sam Duncan and that Cutler kid. That had been messy because of that interfering marshal and Joe had been forced to take the action he had.

Suddenly, Vince turned to face the others.

'C'mon. Let's get back to the Bar. I reckon the old man may have something to say to you two for leaving the Bush woman alive.'

He decided he would say nothing about the stranger at the Benson place.

11

The Silver Spur was unusually quiet. Few people in Progress were in the frame of mind to enjoy a night's drinking. The piano was silent and the saloon girls, without their regular customers, were sitting together at a corner table.

The only other customers were three card players and two lawmen. It was as though the whole town was in mourning for the mayor, gunned down that day in his own home.

Ben McCabe and Corey Hayes had exhausted their conversation. The new young deputy had explained how he had allowed Luther Bush to give him the slip while he was checking on a report — bogus, as it turned out — that there had been a robbery at the general store, and Ben had explained what had happened at the Benson place. So they sat in silence enjoying a beer before they did their rounds and checked on the locks around town.

The barman Sol Dillon was killing time polishing glasses he had already cleaned when he spotted her ... a woman was peering over the batwings and appearing to be searching frantically for a familiar face in the barroom.

Sol had never seen her even walk past the Silver Spur — she was the sort of woman who would cross the street rather than pass in front of a saloon — but he recognized her immediately.

She was his closest neighbour.

'Marshal!' he called out to catch McCabe's attention. 'I reckon you may have a visitor.'

Ben placed his half-finished drink on the table and got to his feet. The deputy made a move to follow but he put his hand on the young man's shoulder.

'You stay here, Corey,' he said quietly. 'The lady looks pretty nervous enough without two of us making things worse.'

McCabe pulled the door towards him and stepped out on to the sidewalk.

'Mrs Duncan. You want to see me?'

The widow of the newspaperman shuffled uncomfortably. She was clearly ill at ease and Ben took hold of her elbow.

'We can go to the office if it would make you feel better,' he suggested.

She nodded. 'I think that would be best, Marshal.'

They crossed the street in silence and it was not until they were inside and she was sitting opposite Ben at his desk that Sarah Duncan appeared to relax. When she spoke her voice was soft, hesitant.

'This isn't easy for me, Marshal and I'm not sure I know where to start,' she said. 'I want you to promise me that that what I am going to say will not make you think that I am being disloyal to my husband's memory.'

It was an easy thing for Ben McCabe to promise. He was hunting the killer of three, maybe four, men. If Sarah Duncan knew something that would throw a light on that he would promise what she wanted. What was a broken promise against the capture of a murderer?

'It will stay between us, Mrs Duncan.'

She nodded, clearly satisfied that the marshal was a man of his word.

'Thank you. I have been married to Sam for almost thirty years. We never had any children; that was Sam's decision. He always said a newspaperman should be devoted to his job and would have no time to help bring up a child and if I wanted children I should marry somebody else.'

Ben sat in silence and listened while the widow told him about her early life, how they had been young lovers in Chicago before Sam set up his own business, ending up here in Progress where he published the *Leader*.

She appeared to be doing her best to avoid the reason she had called on the marshal and Ben was beginning to wonder if she would ever stop extolling the virtues of a young Sam Duncan when she suddenly reached inside the purse she had been carrying over her arm and produced what appeared to be a small notebook.

'I loved Sam, Marshal, and I thought I knew him, but,' she slowly pushed the book across the desk, 'I have decided to leave Progress and go back to my sister's place in Chicago. I was clearing out things that I would not need any more, things that reminded me of Sam, when I came across that.' She pointed to the book. 'I think it might help you find out who killed Sam. And why.'

Ben picked up the notebook and flicked through the pages without reading them. Mrs Duncan rose from her seat to leave but she stopped on her way to the door. 'One more thing, Marshal. It's about the night Sam was killed. I told you he said he had a meeting at the newspaper office and I thought that meeting was with your young deputy, the poor boy who was hanged, because I saw them talking that afternoon.'

'I remember,' Ben said.

'I've been thinking about that a lot, Mr McCabe, and I may have been mistaken. The clothes the man was wearing, they surely looked like the shirt and pants I had seen Mr Cutler wearing around town, except,' she paused before adding, 'except they didn't quite fit the man I saw talking to Sam. It was as though he was wearing clothes that did not belong to him.'

Ben studied the book. The admission by Mrs Duncan that the man she had seen that afternoon might not have been young Cutler after all added weight to Lane's story that he had been held prisoner in a barn and had had his clothes taken away from him before he was released.

Now came this book. The more he read the more he realized that it had taken some courage for the newspaperman's widow to come forward. He would keep that promise he had made.

If ever there was evidence that her husband, the loved and respected owner of the local newspaper, was putting the bite on so many people in Progress it was contained in this book. Sam Duncan had clearly been a meticulous man. At the top of each page was a name and below the name was a list of figures followed by a short, scrawled passage.

Ben turned to the page headed with the name of Lane Cutler. The list of figures ranged from thirty dollars to sixty dollars and below that was the message: Son of Quantrill man Bob Cutler; hiding from law after shooting up in high country. Kid's a fool; seven years on, law's forgotten him. Easy money.

Ben flicked to another page:

Luther Bush. Here there was just one figure: $10,000, and below it was a short, cryptic message: From L and Q when the time comes to talk about rustling and gun-running.

At the top of another page was the name of Billy Jack. More figures, and then the question: What would the lovely Carla think if she knew that her husband ran a whorehouse and regularly sampled the goods?

There were other names on other pages with figures ranging from ten dollars to fifty with notes about gambling, robbery and horse-thieving.

Ben slammed the notebook shut. Sam Duncan had kept these stories out of his newspaper in exchange for money to buy his silence.

Blackmail.

$$\star \quad \star \quad \star$$

Joe Quillan leaned heavily for support on his pearl-handled walking-cane. His leg wound had been giving him more trouble than usual recently, but he regarded that as the least of his worries. The three men who stood in front of him in the expansive room at the front of the ranch house were a much bigger problem.

Jake Lucas was nothing more than a hired cowhand who was useful with a gun, did not ask any questions and did exactly what he was told. Joe expected nothing more from him.

And Zak Hardin: better with cattle than people, was paid well above the normal rate for a ranch foreman because it was his duty to report everything that Vince was up to — whatever and whenever.

'I ain't a nursemaid, Mr Quillan,' Hardin had protested when the ranch owner had told him what he wanted.

'For what I'm paying you, Zak, you'll be what I say you are. I'm not paying you a thousand-dollar bonus just to count beef and fix fences.'

And then there was Vince. Arrogant. Swaggering. His son.

Quillan did not need to ask why Vince had not mentioned the stranger at the Benson place. He knew. Vince never confessed to anything.

Sure, he had silenced the old man and left the ranch in the hands of Benson's daughter, who had lived somewhere out St Louis way and would likely be more than happy to sell to the highest bidder, but who was the stranger? And why had it been left to Hardin to tell the old man about it?

Sometimes he despaired that Vince

would ever amount to anything other than an angry bully. Joe could make him town marshal once they had got rid of McCabe and maybe that would do the trick. But the old man wasn't hopeful.

He raised the cane and pointed it at Hardin.

'So what's your story, Zak? I put you in charge of this and what do I hear? A widow who can tell the law who killed her husband and a stranger who saw Vince shoot Benson. You were supposed to finish this.'

His voice was rising as the anger in him grew. He could see that Vince was enjoying the sight of Hardin facing the anger of the old man. There were too many times when Zak overstepped the mark. Cursing, Joe Quillan dismissed the two hired hands and as soon as they were out of the room he turned on his son.

'Sit down!' he ordered. His tone suggested to Vince that it would be a good idea to obey.

'What is it about you, Vince? Why can't you be like — '

Before he could finish, Vince was back on his feet.

'Like Matt! Ain't that what you were going to say? Well I am not Matt and I'm not like him. And Matt isn't here. It's time you got used to that, old man.'

Picking up his hat he stormed out of the room, leaving his ageing father alone.

Joe Quillan was getting used to being alone.

* * *

Corey Hayes emptied his coffee mug and returned to his chair in the marshal's office. He threw the notebook on to the desk.

'It was a long time ago, Marshal. Lane was only fifteen when it happened. It can't have anything to do with why he was killed.'

Ben tried to hide the exasperation he was feeling when he answered.

'It was the reason he was killed, Corey. Lane may have been a kid when it happened but he did kill somebody and you know about it. Sam Duncan kept the information in that notebook. I want to know about it.'

The young deputy shuffled uncomfortably in his seat. He remembered the day Lane had ridden into the Hayes place and dismounted before the horse had stopped running.

Breathless, he had raced up the steps and dashed into the Hayes house while Corey and his mother were still eating their evening meal.

'Corey! We've got to talk.'

Seeing the distress in his friend's face, Corey had hurried from the table, taken his friend's arm and led him out on to the veranda.

There he had listened to Lane's story of how his father had returned home from the war unexpectedly but on the run from the law. He had been home for only a few days when two bounty hunters came after him.

Lane had helped him to escape but when the two men went after Cutler, Lane tried to slow them down by shooting at them. He hit one. He was pretty sure he had killed him.

'But he was a bounty hunter chasing his father,' Ben protested. 'That's no reason to bury it as a secret.'

'That's all I know, Ben,' Corey said. 'Maybe his death had nothing to do with that. Unless the man he killed was something more than a bounty hunter. A lawman, maybe?'

The two men fell silent until Ben suddenly got to his feet.

'Corey, I reckon that this man Quillan may know the answer. I think it's time we found out more about him and paid him a visit.'

It was late afternoon by the time Ben had established the whereabouts of the Bar-Q, the vast ranch owned by Joe Quillan. It was, he was told, a four-hour ride out of Progress.

'We'll get ourselves a night's sleep in our own beds and set off at first light,' he told his new deputy. He could not have known that the man who had given him directions to the Quillan spread was already halfway there to tell the ranch owner to expect a visit from the law.

Jed Lennon had never liked Ben McCabe.

*   *   *

Joe Quillan threw two ten-dollar bills on to the table and eyed his visitor with contempt. He was under no illusions that Lennon would remain loyal only as long as the money lasted or there was the chance to get Quillan's men to do his dirty work. He was an ugly sight, the bruises and cuts on his face scarring his already sour features. The explanation that the damage had been caused by a young hothead who was asking questions about Lane Cutler stirred the rancher's interest.

'So all you got to tell me is that I'm getting a visit from the town marshal and his new deputy, who gave you a good whipping,' Quillan sneered. 'You don't know why they're coming here or when.'

'Today, Mr Quillan, they're coming today.'

'I pay you for more than that, Lennon. I told you I need somebody in Progress to keep me informed of what's going on in that town and all you come up with is this!'

'Sorry, Mr Quillan,' Lennon offered feebly. 'I just thought you oughta know as soon as I could get here.'

'Right. Well, now you've told me I suggest you pick up your money and get out of here.'

Lennon scooped up the bills, thrust them into his shirt pocket and turned to leave. He had been dismissed. He slouched out of the ranch house and surveyed the scene. Three cowhands were lounging alongside a nearby corral and two more were branding a few of the Bar-Q stock.

Lennon smirked in satisfaction. Those five with Vince and a few others would be more than enough to give that deputy and his boss McCabe what was coming to them; especially the Hayes kid, who had given him the beating. He was still counting the bruises.

The old man had ordered him back to town but he was going nowhere until he had seen them bury the bodies where they would never be found.

Meantime he had to find a spot where he wouldn't be seen. For a long time Jed Lennon had hankered after a job at the Bar-Q. Acting as one of Joe Quillan's spies in Progress had only been a starting point as far as he was concerned. If he stuck around for this showdown with McCabe and the deputy maybe he could be useful enough for Quillan to see he was worth having around for more than just small-town scuttlebutt.

Unnoticed by the group near the corral, Lennon led his horse away from the house and through a small brush where he settled down to await events.

★ ★ ★

'How're we gonna handle this, Ben?'

It was the third time Corey Hayes had asked the question in the last hour and McCabe still did not have an answer. He could hardly ride up to the Bar-Q ranch house and accuse Joe Quillan of a string of killings just because his name had come up. But if Quillan had been involved he would know well enough why the town marshal and his young sidekick were calling.

And this meant that he would see straight through anything McCabe came up with.

'We could play it real neighbourly and invite him to a social in town,' Ben said with a grin, 'or we could tell him why we are paying him a visit.'

The non-reply was enough for Hayes to lapse into silence. He had known Ben McCabe for little more than a day but he had already come to the conclusion that the lawman played his cards close to his chest. He was not the sort of man who liked to share his thoughts with others. But there was more to it than that, this time.

Lane Cutler had been Corey's friend from way back but he had been McCabe's partner and, unless he was wildly mistaken, something of a substitute son. The way McCabe had spoken about Lane it was clear that he had intended to hand over his badge.

Maybe Corey could now be the man to follow him into the marshal's job. But that was for the future. His only concern now was how to handle Quillan. As they approached the gate leading to the Bar-Q, McCabe suddenly held up his hand then leaned forward on to the horn of his saddle.

'Right, Corey, this is what we do from here. There is no reason for both of us to go in.' He held up his hand to halt the first sign of Corey's protest. 'I want you to stay here and wait. If I go in alone, Quillan may just think I am looking for his help. According to George Benson, Luther Bush was Quillan's friend from years ago, so it's only to be expected that I'd be coming looking for his help to find out who killed him.'

Corey Hayes was doubtful.

'From what we hear, Marshal, this man Quillan's no fool. And if he's the one behind Lane's death and maybe those others, he is not going to let you walk out of there.'

Ben chuckled. 'That's a chance I've got to take, Corey, but if I don't come out in an hour you'll know what to do. Get a message to Wichita. The marshal there is an old friend of mine. He'll send either one of his brothers to see that Quillan gets what's coming to him.'

Before Corey could protest further Ben was heading through the gates that signalled the start of the Quillan ranch.

He was not certain that he was doing the right thing but it was a chance he had to take. The longer the mystery surrounding the deaths of Lane Cutler, Sam Duncan, Luther Bush and George Benson went on, the harder it would be for Ben to come up with evidence against the man he believed to have had a hand in those killings.

The road leading to the ranch house stretched ahead of him but there was no sign of any cowhands until he reached the corral. A group of men were idling their time away while others were throwing horseshoes at the pike and gambling away their wages.

One of the men lounging against the corral fence stepped out in front of Ben's horse. The marshal had a vague recollection of seeing the man around town occasionally but had never had reason to speak to him as far as he could remember. He pulled his horse to a halt and the ranch hand reached up to grab the reins.

'Hello, Marshal. You're a long ways from home.'

Ben was in no mood to exchange pleasantries with the hired help and pulled sharply on the reins, forcing the horse's head back and the Bar-Q man to stumble forward and release his grip.

'Are you the boss?'

'Ranch foreman, Marshal. Zak Hardin. What can I do for you?'

Ben dismounted. 'You could call the boss. That would be a help.'

Hardin stood his ground, aware that the lazing cowhands were watching him.

'Well, I ain't sure that he's home right now, Marshal.'

'Yes you are. Now you either get him out to see me or I go up to the house. I am not too bothered which it is.'

Hardin glanced across at the others. This was turning into a stand-off and the foreman was quick to realize that it was one he was not going to win.

'Go ahead, Marshal. I was just trying to be friendly. Mr Quillan is up at the house though I ain't sure he'll see you.'

'I'm trying to be friendly too, Mr Hardin. And he will see me.'

Ben pushed past the foreman and led his horse to the hitching rail at the bottom of the steps leading to the house. At the top he came face to face with the man he had ridden to meet.

Joe Quillan, brown town suit and pearl-handled cane just as Lane had remembered, stretched out his hand in

169

welcome and McCabe took it. But there was no warmth in the handshake, nor in the smile that accompanied it.

'Marshal McCabe. What brings you out to the Bar-Q? Can't say I remember seeing you this way before. I hope none of my boys have been stepping out of line in Progress. If they've been causing trouble I'll take it out of their wages.'

'No, I think I can deal with drunken cowhands, Mr Quillan, but judging by your question I reckon you may not have heard. Luther Bush has been murdered.'

Ben waited for a response from the ranch owner but none came other than a puzzled frown across the craggy features.

Eventually Quillan said: 'You came some thirty miles out here to tell me that, Marshal? Why would you do that?'

'Two reasons. First my information is that the mayor was a friend of yours and I thought you'd like to know that a friend had been killed in his own house.'

'Well, I thank you for that, but I don't

know who told you that Luther Bush was my friend. Sure, I knew him, but that was a long time ago. We arrived in Progress County around the same time but that was close to twenty years ago.

'I don't reckon I've seen or spoken to him more than ten times in all those years. No, Marshal, I'm sorry to say you've had a long ride out here for nothing. The fact that Luther Bush has been shot doesn't concern me, least-ways not unless you're about to accuse one of my men of killing him.'

Ben let the suggestion linger in the air before he said: 'No, nothing like that — at least, not yet or until I get some evidence.'

'You said there were two reasons. What was the other one?'

McCabe rubbed his chin as if deep in thought. 'I reckon that don't matter much now. If Luther Bush wasn't a friend of yours, you won't know of anybody who might want to kill him. Somebody from his past, maybe?'

'Sorry, Marshal. Twenty years is a

long time, but' — he paused to light a cigar and blow clouds of smoke in Ben's direction — 'I don't understand.'

'Well, only a few days ago my young deputy, Lane Cutler, was hanged out at the Benson place. It looked to me like some kind of revenge killing and I thought it might be linked with Luther's shooting. I suppose it was a wild hunch, coming here, but I'm running out of ideas and I was told not much happens in these parts without Joe Quillan's knowing or say-so. So here I am. But like you say, it looks like I've had a long ride for nothing.'

'I don't know who told you that I know everything that happens around here. I am just a rancher. Sure, I've got a big spread with more head of cattle than I can count, but what goes on outside my range I leave for people like yourself to worry about.'

Ben rose from his comfortable arm-chair and made to leave, but when he reached the door he paused and turned.

'There's one other thing, Mr Quillan. If you hadn't heard about Luther

Bush's killing you won't have heard that we've had another murder in Progress. A relative of yours. George Benson.'

Quillan lowered his cigar.

'Now that *is* bad news, Marshal. George was a good man. He was married to my sister, you know. How did he get it?'

'Bushwhacked on his own veranda. I was there when it happened. We were putting the finishing touches to a deal we'd made. I was going to buy the Benson place and I was there to tell him that his money was on the way.'

Quillan took another long puff on his cigar.

'Did you see who shot him?'

'No, I didn't. But I'll find him, I promise you that.'

He put on his Stetson and turned to leave.

'Like I said, George was a good man, so I hope you find his killer, Marshal.'

Why is it that I don't believe you? Ben thought as he remounted his horse and headed for the glade where he had left Corey Hayes. The journey had not been such a waste after all. The seeds of doubt had been sown in Joe Quillan's mind.

Lane's description of the man who had held him captive in an abandoned barn fitted the suited ranch owner perfectly. Ben was convinced he was behind the killing of Lane Cutler. What he didn't know was, why? And what had the killings of newspaperman Sam Duncan, Mayor Luther Bush and small-time rancher George Benson got to do with Lane's hanging?

The lawman was convinced that the answers lay around the Bar-Q. Or 'the Bar' as Lane had heard one of his tormentors — the one called Vince — call it. That was another problem for the marshal of Progress. Who was Vince?

★ ★ ★

Jed Lennon lowered his spyglass and scowled. Hidden well out of view from the road, he had watched Quillan and McCabe go into the big house together and then, barely ten minutes later, the lawman emerged alone, remounted his horse and rode slowly away just like he had been calling on an old friend.

What was happening? He had warned the old man that McCabe was going to pay him a visit, even hinted that the marshal suspected something, yet there he was, large as life, riding away from the Bar-Q as though he did not have a care in the world.

Lennon lay in his hideaway and watched McCabe rejoin that young kid, Hayes. The two men chatted briefly before heading off along the road and out of sight.

Jed was powerless to do anything about it other than let his limited imagination run riot. Why had old man Quillan allowed the man with the badge to ride away free? He knew that would not have happened if Vince had been around instead of out on the range fixing fences or such. By now Jed would be helping to find a good place to bury the two lawmen. There were times when Lennon thought that Quillan was showing signs of his age; it was high time he handed things over to Vince, who was Lennon's sort of guy.

His thoughts were interrupted by a sound from somewhere over to his left. He stiffened, his hand closing around the butt of his gun. Lennon was no gunman. In fact, he had only ever been called upon to draw once in his life and he had survived that only because the man facing him was too drunk to shoot straight. Jed was not afraid of trouble so long as he was on the outside looking in. Right now, it seemed as though he was getting closer to the inside.

He rolled over on to his elbow, prepared to release his Colt from its holster. But he was too slow. He looked up into the bright sunlight, his eyes unable to focus on the tall figure who emerged from the bushes. All he could make out was the barrel of a rifle pointed at his chest.

'You know something, Jed? I reckon you are becoming a bit of a problem.'

Lennon did not need to see the face.

The voice was enough.

'Oh, it's you. I — I am only looking after your interests,' he stammered, releasing the grip on his gun butt. 'I told the old man that McCabe was coming. I told him — '

'I know what you told him, Jed. You told him that you thought the marshal suspected something to connect the Bar-Q with that young deputy's killing.'

'That's right. I did.' Lennon relaxed. But only briefly.

'The thing is, Jed, why did he suspect something? Who's been talking out of turn and giving the marshal these ideas about us? The trouble is the old man . . . well, he's old. He is past doing things the way the Quillans are used to. If you want it — take it.'

The rifle remained steadily pointed at Lennon's chest.

'You know something else, Jed? You have been very useful through all of this. You told us all about young Cutler, you even told us that that double-crossing mayor was about to run out.'

Lennon was still feeling nervous at the sight of the rifle still pointed at him, but he managed to find his voice.

'I've been paid and the old man — er, Mr Quillan — he said I've been doing a good job.'

The man with the rifle sniggered. 'And we are grateful to you for that, we surely are. But I've been watching you lately and when you've got a drink inside you, you talk too much and you know how loose talk leads to more trouble. You can see that, can't you, Jed? How are we to know that it wasn't your drink talk that gave McCabe his suspicions about the Bar-Q? He's been here three years without paying us a visit and now, suddenly, he's interested in us.'

Lennon was frightened. There was a coldness in the voice and he had experienced it before and seen the consequences.

'I would never say anything to bring a lawman down on the Bar-Q. You must know that. Besides I don't know anything — '

He got no further. Vince Quillan squeezed

the trigger of the rifle and fired into the chest of the man for no other reason than the one that had ruled his life.

'I never did like you, Jed Lennon,' he said, turning away and leaving the town gossip to breathe his last.

* * *

Corey Hayes threw another stone into the creek and shook his head. The two Progress lawmen had stopped to give their horses a rest halfway though their ride back to town. The marshal had been unusually quiet and Corey's attempts to learn what had happened at the meeting with the owner of the Bar-Q had brought nothing more helpful than the occasional grunt. In the end he had given up and the journey continued in silence.

Corey's only interest when he arrived in Progress had been to help find the killer of his friend Lane Cutler.

But all that had changed in the past few days. He was now a deputy marshal and his job was to help Ben McCabe discover the identity of whoever had killed newspaperman Sam Duncan, Luther Bush, the mayor of Progress and George Benson, who had been gunned down while talking over the sale of his ranch to the marshal. And still they did not know who had killed Lane. Four killings . . . and the only name to connect them was Quillan.

Frustrated, he hurled another stone into the creek and turned to face McCabe, who had settled under a tree while the horses grazed near by.

'Marshal, if you don't want to tell me what went on back there why bring me along?'

'Because you insisted,' Ben told him. 'I asked you to stay in town.'

Corey didn't argue and turned away. Ben got to his feet and dusted himself down. 'But now you are here I reckon you are entitled to know how things are.'

Corey listened without interruption while the older man outlined his suspicions of how it had all started with the killing of Sam Duncan and the imprisonment of Lane Cutler.

'As soon as I met Quillan today I knew that Lane had been held prisoner by the old man. He described him perfectly, including the town suit and the walking-cane. Which meant he was telling the truth about not being in town when Mrs Duncan said she saw him talking to her husband. He didn't kill the newspaperman.'

He paused and took his turn to throw a loose stone into the creek.

'Whoever killed Sam Duncan wanted us to believe it was Lane, but why? What had Lane done to make somebody arrange a vengeance killing? Lane was hanged, and unless I'm mistaken the deaths of Luther Bush and George Benson are linked with the hanging. And Joe Quillan has something to do with it all.'

Ben fell silent again, suddenly realizing that he was just thinking aloud.

'The answer is back there at the

Bar-Q,' he said at last. 'Trouble is, Corey, I've got no evidence to back up anything I've said. Somebody at the Bar-Q killed Lane. I'm sure of it. And even though I don't know why or how, it all ties up with the other killings, starting with Sam Duncan.'

Corey looked at him uncomfortably. 'So what are you planning to do?'

'I got to thinking while we were riding back and I can't see how I've got a lot of choice. I've got to let the Bar-Q know I'm on to them. I've got to get them to come to me.'

'And how are you going to do that?'

'The man who set fire to the newspaper building and killed Sam Duncan left that deputy's badge as evidence against Lane. I need something to tie the Bar-Q with Luther, Lane, Sam and maybe even George Benson. Right now, I don't know how I'm going to do that, but by the time we get back to Progress I hope to come up with an idea.

'Let's mount up. It's time to get back to town. I have a telegram to send to an old friend of mine. He may be interested to hear that there's a Zak Hardin working with the Bar-Q outfit.'

★　★　★

Joe Quillan sat alone in the darkness. The visit from the Progress marshal was the last thing he needed. There were times when he felt he could happily leave Vince to sort out his own mess. He had been a handful for most of his twenty-six years, driven by a cruel streak since his schooldays, and things had got steadily worse since his mother died. Although Joe could handle situations such as the occasional drunken brawl — though even they had become too regular lately — the old man could not close his mind to other instances of Vince's lawbreaking.

There had been two shootings that Joe knew about, but he had managed to keep Vince out of jail in the past with the help of Luther Bush and an ageing town marshal looking for an easy life and a few extra dollars to sustain him in his later years.

But, unlike old Frank Chester before him, McCabe was not the sort of lawman who would let sleeping dogs lie, and the small price to pay was to keep Vince out of Progress. The fact that he had to do his whoring and drinking in Baxterville, the one-horse town near the Missouri border, and the occasional visit across the river into St Joseph meant that he was within reaching distance of the woman he had set his sights on for the future. A Mary Seabrooke, according to Zak.

But Hardin was becoming worse than useless at keeping Vince in line and now there were more killings. Luther Bush and George Benson had to be added to the list.

Joe could understand and maybe even approve the killing of Mayor Bush because the double-crosser was threatening to run out on them and take the gold and cash with him. But George Benson? He was just an old man, like

Joe himself, so what threat could he have been?

Vince was out of control. As Joe toyed with his late-night whiskey and flicked the ash off the end of his cigar he just stared into the blackness around him. Soon that blackness would become total. Joe Quillan's eyesight was failing rapidly. Within a few months he would be blind and the Bar-Q would be in the hands of Vince and his sidekicks.

Maybe that was the reason for killing old George: Vince would not be happy with just the Bar-Q. He would want the whole range.

Joe fumbled for the whiskey bottle, refilled his glass and settled back into the comfort of his well-padded armchair. As he slumped back his thoughts strayed to the day he'd arrived in the remote town of Progress.

Progress. Strange name for a town that consisted of nothing more than a row of houses, a hotel, a saloon, a broken-down general store that had long since been boarded up and an unfinished church that, like the store, had been abandoned and left to rot.

'You're sure this is the right place, darling?'

Quillan remembered the disbelief on his wife's face and the look of excitement in the eyes of his young sons as they raced along the sidewalk towards another of the empty buildings, the marshal's office, after the stage pulled up outside the hotel.

The only other passenger on the Wichita-bound stage was a man of his own age, of heavier build and rugged features, but with a ready smile, who had kept the boys amused ever since the start of the journey. Card tricks and tunes on his mouth harp had made it a happy group.

'Maybe it will be better than it looks, Mrs Quillan,' the passenger suggested. 'After all, even the biggest trees start from the smallest seeds.'

Joe Quillan and his fellow traveller had kept up the pretence that they were strangers throughout the journey and it

186

was only when they shared a drink afterwards that he and Luther Bush were able to renew an association that had started many years earlier . . . a relationship that made both of them rich. In the years after the Mexican War of 1848 they had been partners: two men who lived outside the law, part of a group of deserters that formed themselves into a gang of stage robbers, and from there they headed to the goldfields of California. Even after the break-up of the Casey Gang they dodged the law in Nevada and Colorado before going legal in Kansas. It was a lucrative partnership that was to end twenty years later when Vince, once so enthralled by a stranger's magic tricks on a long stage journey, had become an out-of-control killer.

Finishing his cigar, Joe struggled to his feet, thought about and then discarded the idea of another drink, and with the support of his cane hobbled across the floor towards the staircase. The headache could have been caused by the drink, but he doubted it. He was getting them even when he wasn't drinking. Slowly he made his way up the stairs and into his room at the far end of the house. Along the passage Vince would be sleeping soundly after another heavy night's drinking. His conscience would not be keeping him awake.

Tomorrow was another day and for Vince that meant life would go on as normal. But for Joe Quillan it was another day closer to blindness.

* * *

The old man was wrong about Vince. He was not sleeping off another night of heavy drinking. The bed in the room along the passage was empty.

Digging a hole deep enough to bury that big-mouthed scuttlebutt Jed Lennon had been thirsty work, but the thought of another night in some small-town barroom had no appeal. Besides, he was getting tired of being told where he could not go and treated as though he needed a nursemaid. If he had to have one he would have chosen somebody a lot better-looking than Zak Hardin. What was the old man thinking about? Had he gone soft in the head?

Much of the searing heat had gone from the sun as it started its slow descent in the western sky, but Vince felt the need for strong drink growing with every minute. With St Joseph off his list for the time being, there was only one other town within a four-hour ride and that was the one place that was off limits. Well, not any more. Hardin was nowhere to be seen and what he didn't know he could not report back to the old man. Vince threw his shovel into the bushes, mounted his horse and headed off towards Progress.

Throughout the ride his mind wandered back to the last time he had visited the town. He had stood alongside Hardin under the cover of darkness and watched as the townsfolk panicked at the sight of their newspaper office all ablaze. Nobody had seen him then; the Cutler kid was history and he had nothing to worry about now. Even that town marshal had no idea who he was so he could look forward to a night's gambling and drinking in the saloon before finding himself a woman. Vince was in a good mood when, shortly after sunset, he drew his horse to a halt outside the Regal Palace hotel and crossed the street to the Silver Spur.

The saloon was quiet when Vince pushed his way through the batwings, glanced around and then strode purposefully towards the bar.

'Whiskey and leave the bottle. None of your rotgut stuff.'

'Sorry, mister. First things first. I'll need that gun.'

Vince leaned on the bar and stared into the face of Sol Dillon, the world-weary barman.

'Who says so?'

'Look, mister. It's the law. Guns have got to be checked in before I can serve liquor. You get it back when you leave. Don't blame me. If you got any problems see the town marshal.'

Vince scowled. McCabe. Another good reason to see that the lawman did not reach old age. But that was for some other time. Right now he needed a drink and if that meant handing over his gun-belt then that was what he would do.

'What does a man do in this town for entertainment?' he asked, sliding the belt across the bar and throwing his coins carelessly towards Sol.

'It's early yet. Things will get a bit more to your liking later on when the girls come on duty and the card-players get in.'

Vince snatched up the whiskey bottle and glass and headed for one of the empty tables across the room.

He was on his third glass when he got the first signs that the Silver Spur would be livening up. The dancing girls put in an appearance and a pianist started to tune up. But, just as important for Vince, the card-players were settling into their seats.

There were four of them, all several

years older than Vince himself and all, he guessed, were easy pickings. The visit to Progress was not going to be so quiet after all.

* * *

Carla Jack was serving the last of the Little Lady café's customers but she was in no hurry to close up for the night. She did not often get the chance to talk about things other than steaks, stews or newly baked bread, but Marshal McCabe and his new young deputy offered something more than chatter about life over a kitchen stove.

They were just finishing the last of their suppers, which had been eaten in almost total, grim-faced silence, when Carla moved in to start clearing their table.

'You two look as though you have lost ten dollars and found ten cents,' she said, sliding into one of the empty seats. 'Anything a mere woman can do to help?'

Ben emptied his cup before answering.

'I'm not sure there is a way to help, Carla, not unless you have got any ideas on how the law can arrest a man for murder without any proof.'

Carla sighed. 'Don't know about that, Marshal. You got anybody particular in mind?'

Before Ben could answer, Corey interrupted: 'We reckon we know who killed Lane and maybe Sam Duncan, too. Trouble is, it's only a feeling. No evidence.'

Carla refilled their coffee cups.

'I see your problem, but that's the best I can do — another coffee.'

She moved away and left Ben and Corey to their discussion. An hour later they were back at the office but no closer to a solution.

'The way I see it, Ben, is that we agree that the Bar-Q is where Lane was held prisoner and that's where we will find his killer, but we can't just walk in there and drag old Joe out by his collar.'

Ben smiled. 'You're right there. All we've got is Lane's description and something Sam Duncan said to Luther.'

'The dead newspaperman?'

Ben nodded. 'Luther told me Sam mentioned the name in connection with Lane. Sam was drunk at the time and Luther said he didn't understand what he meant. Now I'm not so sure. Those two knew each other from long ago. Tomorrow I will pay Martha Bush a visit; maybe she might have some answers. But I'm feeling worn out and could use a good night's sleep. I don't think there is anything else we can do tonight.'

He was wrong.

Across the street Vince was in a sour mood. The cards had been falling badly all night and he was halfway down the second bottle of whiskey.

He studied his latest hand: two threes, a seven, a four and a ten. A nothing hand. He had had too many of them for one night. He refilled his glass.

'You playin', mister?'

The dealer, a man who, he vaguely

remembered, had introduced himself as Fred Adams, the town stable and bath-house owner, paused, waiting for Vince's call.

'Three!' Vince snapped, throwing in three cards. 'And take them off the top of the deck this time.'

Fred Adams hesitated again. 'What are you saying, mister? You saying I'm cheating you?'

'I'm saying I've handed over a lot of money tonight and that don't fit too good with me. I aim to win it back.'

Vince snatched up his new cards and studied them without a flicker of movement in his stony features. The genuine poker face. His new hand gave him a full house of three threes and two queens.

Two of the players quickly dropped out and were followed by Fred Adams. That left Vince and a man he knew to be the town's barber, Dick Kyle. Gradually the pile of notes in the middle of the table grew and with it the tension built. The pianist stopped playing and an unnatural quiet fell over the room.

Eventually it came to the showdown, Vince grinning as he shoved his five cards on to the table. But the grin disappeared when Kyle revealed his hand: four kings and one of the remaining queens.

Nobody spoke. Vince took a long slug of his whiskey and got to his feet. Suddenly, with barely the slightest sign of movement, he reached behind his back, withdrew a knife and plunged it into the pile of notes.

'Leave it!' Vince snapped. 'We ain't finished yet.'

'Now look here, mister — '

Fred Adams's outburst got no further. Vince swung his free left hand across the side of the older man's face, a smack that sent him reeling from his chair and crashing into the piano.

Kyle moved forward, but before he could act Vince reached down to his boot and produced another weapon, a derringer pocket pistol.

'Like I said, we ain't finished,' Vince snarled. 'We got one more hand to play.'

'You lost fair and square.'

Vince sneered back at Kyle's challenge.

'Then let's just say I'm a bad loser. Now sit.'

'The hell — '

Vince raised the derringer and fired into Kyle's shoulder, sending the barber spinning backwards, clutching the wound.

'Bastard!'

Leaning forward, Vince pulled the knife out of the bills and stuffed the money into his shirt pocket.

'You'll live,' he said coldly.

All around him the Silver Spur customers backed away.

'That's fine, folks. Just stay where you are and you'll all go home to your beds safely.' Taking another swig of the whiskey, he made his way towards the bar. 'My gun, bartender. I'm leaving.'

Dillon slid the gunbelt across the bar.

Unnoticed, Fred Adams had staggered to his feet. Without warning he raced across the floor and lunged at the man who had swatted him aside like an annoying fly. Rage blinded him to reason or fear of any consequences and it was the reckless impulse of a man who was more than twice Quillan's age. Even so, he managed to catch the younger man off balance and the pair collapsed in a heap.

Swinging blindly, Adams caught Vince on the side of the chin, but it was a feeble gesture.

'You crazy fool,' Vince barked, pushing the older man aside. But Adams refused to release his hold and the two men grappled for several seconds, rolling over the floor while others tried to pull them apart.

But the struggle came to a sudden stop, halted by the sound of a gunshot. Fred Adams's body stiffened. There was a stunned silence, broken only when Vince pushed the burly figure off him and got to his feet. His shirt front was stained with the blood of Adams, who lay motionless at his feet.

As if suddenly aware that he was facing an attack from a mob, Vince backed away.

Turning, he burst out of the saloon, raced across the street and was on his horse in a matter of seconds. The customers crowded around the supine figure of Fred Adams. Sol Dillon felt for signs of life.

'Get the doc, he's still breathing. And somebody tell Marshal McCabe what's happened.'

A customer ran off to find the doctor. Pop Danton, the ageing pianist who had been a stunned spectator throughout the incident, offered: 'I'll go for the marshal, Sol. Though I'm thinking he ain't gonna want to know.'

'What you saying, Pop? Why wouldn't he want to know that Fred has been shot and Dick Kyle's got a bullet in him?'

'You don't know who that was, do you, Sol?'

His question went unanswered.

'His old man's the richest and most powerful fella around these parts. That guy who just ran out of here was Joe Quillan's son, Vince.'

★ ★ ★

It was well after midnight and the town was in total darkness. Except for the marshal's office, where Ben McCabe was trying to keep a crowd of angry citizens in order.

'It was Vince Quillan sure enough, Marshal. I remember the day old Frank Chester warned him to stay out of town a few years back. He ain't been seen around these parts in a long time. He's no good, Mr McCabe — just like his old man.'

Pop Danton was enjoying the attention. The marshal's office was crowded with customers who had been in the saloon when Vince picked his fight and shot the two card-players, Dick Kyle and Fred Adams, three hours earlier.

'You're gonna arrest him, Marshal? Ain't that your duty?' asked Kyle, who had had his arm strapped up and was now wearing a sling.

'You got plenty of witnesses who saw him shoot Dick here and old Fred,' said the barman.

'Yeah, don't forget Fred Adams.'

Ben did not know where that came from but he had no intention of forgetting Fred, who was now lying in the doctor's surgery with his life in the balance.

'If you're looking for men to make up a posse, Marshal, you can count me in.'

Again, Ben could only guess where the voice came from but he chose to ignore it. Posses had been known to turn into shooting parties, or even worse, lynch mobs, at the first chance they got and he needed to get Vince Quillan in front of a judge before he stood at the end of a rope.

'Now, listen, all of you.' Ben could feel the anger rising. 'At first light Corey and me will ride out to the Quillan place and bring Vince in to face a judge. If he's not there, then we might talk about getting a posse together. Now, you all go home and leave this to the law.'

'It looks as though the law ain't handling it too well up to now, Marshal.'

A tall man in a black shirt and vest

had pushed his way through the crowd and stood, thumbs in his belt and legs slightly apart, in front of the lawman. He was an imposing figure.

'And who are you?' Corey Hayes asked.

'My name's not important, Deputy, but it seems to me there's been a few too many killings around Progress just lately. Sam Duncan, Lane Cutler, Luther Bush, George Benson . . . that's quite a list.'

Corey studied the stranger. He had never seen him around town and he looked to be much more than just a drifter passing through.

'And what's your interest?' Corey asked. 'You don't look to me like a concerned citizen.'

The man chuckled. 'Maybe I don't. I don't want you to think I'm here just to stir up trouble, but word gets around.'

The crowd studied the new face among them. He was a handsome man. Clean-shaven with deep-blue eyes and a strong jaw. When he spoke it was with a voice of authority.

'Look, Marshal. We can talk here in front of all these people, or you can do as you say and send everybody home. Then we can talk.'

Ben decided. 'All right, folks, you heard the man. There's nothing for you to see here. Go on home and leave this to us.'

Slowly, reluctantly, the crowd dispersed. Pop Danton was the last to leave. At the door he turned.

'I wish you luck, Mr McCabe. The Quillans are a mighty powerful family.'

He closed the door quietly and Ben stood face to face with the man who had just walked back into his life. Corey Hayes could only stand and stare as the two men wrapped their arms around each other in a bear hug embrace of two old friends.

When they eventually separated Ben turned to his new deputy, his features cracked into a wide grin.

'I want you to meet one of the people who saved my life ten years ago. Corey Hayes, meet US Marshal Tommy Kane.'

12

'The Quillans must be a bad lot, Ben. Anybody who hires Zak Hardin is hiring trouble.'

McCabe nodded. 'I've seen the Wanted bill and when I found him working out at the Bar-Q I sent for you. Rustling and stage robbery up in Montana are a bit outside the jurisdiction of a small-town marshal heading for retirement.'

'And Kansas and Missouri,' Tommy offered. 'And there's every likelihood that he was involved in a shooting.'

'Just the job for a government lawman.' Ben grinned. 'Aren't you sorry you didn't stick to farming?'

Tommy Kane sipped his coffee. 'As you know, little brother Josh was always the farming type. When Grandpa died and mother went off with that new husband of hers, me and Ellie decided to move on. She's got her own ladies' store in Winfield and the kids — '

'Kids? None of your letters ever mentioned kids.'

'Twins. Elspeth, after Mother, and — er — Benjamin.'

'Benjamin?'

'We call him Ben.'

McCabe fell silent.

'Don't look so surprised. If it wasn't for you I could be singing with the angels. You saved me from the rope, remember?'

'You could also be ploughing fields for a living instead of leaving a wife and children back home while you chase around the country after no-good outlaws like Hardin.'

'Maybe so, but here I am and apart from that list of dead men I got out of the talkative desk clerk in the hotel earlier, all I know about your troubles is what you said in your telegram.'

Ben refilled the coffee cups and, with a little help from Corey Hayes, he filled in the details.

When he had finished, his friend got up from his seat and paced the office.

'From what you say, you think the killings are all connected and this man Sam Duncan was being paid to keep silent about things he knew. Seems to me that a lot of people came to this town with something they wanted to keep quiet. They saw Progress as some kind of hideaway where their secrets would be safe.'

'And Sam Duncan knew about most of them,' Corey put in.

Tommy Kane nodded. 'And it's what cost him his life. But how do the others fit in? Why would the Quillans take your young deputy prisoner, then release him, and where did the mayor and that George Benson fit in?'

The trio were still mulling over the problem when the office door suddenly opened and Doc Miller entered the room. One look at his face was enough to tell Ben that it was bad news.

'Fred Adams just died, Marshal.'

Ben and Tommy exchanged glances

and Corey Hayes shook his head.

'There's no mystery about this one, Marshal. Vince Quillan is our man and no mistake.'

'You're right about that, Corey. No mistake, so I suggest we all get a few hours' sleep and then head for the Bar-Q at first light. But remember, I don't expect Joe Quillan to give up his son easily, or even if he does that Vince will come along quietly.'

'Then we'll just have to bring him in the other way,' said Tommy. 'And he'll have Zak Hardin to keep him company.'

*   *   *

Shortly before daybreak Vince Quillan reined his tired horse to a halt and hurried into the main house at the Bar-Q. It was time to get out. He was sure those damn fool card-players deserved what they'd got, just like Jed Lennon — but the lawman McCabe would not see it that way. He'd be after blood and it was a sure thing that he would be heading for the Bar-Q come daylight. *Well, he won't find me here,* Vince mused. Of course, he could stay and face the lawman but McCabe would not come alone. And he doubted if he could call on that two-faced Judas of a ranch foreman to stand by his shoulder. As for the rest, they were just the hired help and would not want to get involved.

The time was right to run until the heat died down.

Vince had reached the foot of the stairs and was about to go to his room to collect the $1,000 he had stashed away for such an emergency when, from out of the darkness, came a voice that stopped him in his tracks.

'Vince? That you?'

He turned and despite the poor light, he could make out the shape of a figure in a chair in the far corner of the room.

'Pa. What you doing sitting there in the dark?'

'Waiting for you, son. Just waiting for you.'

Joe Quillan's voice was even but without warmth. He had been unable to sleep and had stumbled into Vince's room hoping to have a father-to-son talk about the future of the Bar-Q. Only when he found that the bed was empty did he know that trouble would not be far away.

'Where've you been all night?' he asked, his tone still cold.

Vince bristled. What was the old man going to complain about this time?

'I've just been having a few drinks, Pa. And a hand or two of cards. What's wrong?'

'In Baxterville?'

'Sure. Where else?'

Joe Quillan felt the anger that had been simmering during the five hours he had been sitting in the darkness waiting for his son's return now rising.

'If you're going to lie to me at least get somebody to back up your lies.'

Joe struggled to his feet and ambled slowly towards Vince.

'I know you weren't in Baxterville.

Zak's been there.'

'Zak! Zak! It's always Zak,' Vince snapped. 'Right — so I wasn't in Baxterville. You know where I was, Pa? I was in Progress. I was playing cards and getting drunk.' His voice was rising. 'I had to get away from Zak. And from you. And from the Bar-Q. I'm my own man, Pa. I don't need a nursemaid.'

Suddenly, Joe Quillan lost what was left of his temper. Raising his cane, he lashed out and caught Vince across the shoulder. But the bigger, younger man barely flinched. Instead, he grabbed the cane and snatched it from his father's grasp. Staring coldly into his father's face, he barked:

'That's the first and last time you ever use that on me.' Snapping the cane across his knee he threw the two pieces into the far corner of the room. He grabbed his father's lapels and pulled the old man towards him, the rage in his eyes clearly visible even to Joe Quillan's fading vision.

Fury overruled what was left of

Vince's reason. Strengthening his grip on his father's shirt, he shook the old man violently, throwing him across the room and sending the drinks table crashing against the wall. Joe Quillan thudded against the armchair and rolled into a heap, curling up in an effort to protect himself from his son.

'I've warned you, Pa. Never try that again.'

He stepped over his father, turned and hurried up the staircase. Minutes later, his rucksack stuffed with shirts and pants and his pockets full of money, he ran down the stairs. His father was crouched on the floor. Vince ignored the forlorn figure. He bounded out of the house and away from the Bar-Q.

Inside the house, Joe Quillan rose to his feet and slumped into his armchair. Wiping his tired and failing eyes he stared into the darkness and doubted that he would ever see his son again.

★　★　★

211

Three riders approached the large gates leading to the Bar-Q and pulled their mounts to a halt. The morning sun, which cast long shadows from the tall trees on either side of the road leading to the ranch, was already warm.

The trio dismounted and Tommy Kane studied the surroundings. Ben saw the frown form across his young friend's face.

'Big spread,' he said, putting Tommy's thoughts into words. 'Our men will not be too easy to find.'

'And they won't come in without a fight,' Corey put in. The others nodded in agreement. 'Are you ready for a shoot-out, Ben?'

'If that's what it takes,' McCabe agreed, 'but . . . ' He paused. 'Bringing in Vince Quillan for killing Fred Adams isn't enough, Tommy. I've got to know if he was behind the hanging of Lane Cutler and the other killings. And I've got to know why.'

'You want him alive,' Kane said quietly.

'That's it. He's no good to me if we take him back to Progress face down over a horse.'

Without another word the three lawmen remounted and headed towards the ranch house. None of them saw the man perched high on the ridge to the south side of the Bar-Q.

Cole Jennings slid from his perch on the rock and down the hillside to his waiting horse in the valley. Zak Hardin wanted to know about any visitors calling on the old man. He would be interested to hear of the arrival of the two lawmen from Progress and the tall young stranger in black.

* * *

Joe Quillan had lived the life of a hard-bitten outlaw, a ruthless rancher and a callous cattle dealer unhindered at all times by any feeling for his fellow man. Even the death of his wife at the hands of some incompetent doctor had failed to evoke any signs of emotion.

213

When his favourite son was shot down in his youth, leaving Vince as the only remaining family member to carry on what he hoped would one day be a Quillan dynasty, the only emotion he had expressed was anger. There was never any sign of what he would have described as weakness: sorrow at the loss of a loved one. Ever since that day he had abandoned even the pretence of any benevolence he had allowed to spread among the people of Progress County and beyond.

Joe devoted his life to making the Bar-Q the biggest and richest ranch in the territory, to putting his old friend Luther Bush into the state senate and giving Vince the chance to show that he was the man to carry on the Quillan empire. He now knew that that had been a big mistake. Luther had turned against him, had even allowed the Quillan name to be dragged into the death of that newspaperman Sam Duncan — and Vince was a cold-blooded thug and killer.

Maybe that was his fault, too. After

all, Vince did have his father's blood running through his veins.

Joe had never believed he was heading for sainthood. From his youth down in Texas and through his marriage and fatherhood, Joe's only recognition of right and wrong was that the rich were always right. And he would be rich one day.

But when that day had come it had arrived at a price. His eyesight was fading fast and his son had attacked him and fled from the house. Now, as he toyed with the two broken pieces of his favourite walking-cane that would forever be a reminder of the day his son turned on him, he was faced with the three lawmen who were demanding to know the whereabouts of Vince and his foreman, Zak Hardin.

And they had brought with them the news that Vince had killed a man in Progress only the night before.

'That can't be, McCabe,' he protested. 'Vince was here all night. He never left the house.'

Ben studied the old man. There was fear in those failing eyes. Joe Quillan knew that the law had not ridden all this way on a hunch. They had the proof that had so often eluded them in the past.

'You know that's not true, Quillan. He spent his night drinking and gambling in the Silver Spur. We have a whole barroom full of people who saw him pick a fight with two of the saloon's regulars. He accused one of them of cheating and he shot both. One died. And your son killed him.'

The old man slumped back into his favourite armchair where he had spent the hours since Vince rode off. He knew the marshal was telling the truth.

'Where is he, Joe?'

Joe Quillan was a beaten man. Broken.

'He's gone, Marshal. He rode out a few hours ago.' He held up his hand. 'Don't ask me where. I don't know. And if I did I wouldn't tell you. Vince is all I got left and even if he did kill that man like you say I'm sure it was self-defence and I would not turn him over to you.'

'Both men were unarmed, unlike your son, who pulled out a hand pistol, a derringer, from his boot. We'll find him and when we do I don't want to shoot him down like some mad dog. But there's every chance that might happen. Do you want that on your conscience?'

Conscience? Was old Joe Quillan ever going to find that he had a conscience?

'Like I said, Marshal, Vince is all I got and you can't have him — not from me.'

Corey Hayes spoke for the first time. There was anger in his voice. He stepped forward and leaned close to Joe's face.

'Now you listen to me, old man. Your son's a mean, cold-blooded bastard and I'm not as law-abiding as Marshal McCabe. I'm here for one reason only. I think your son hanged my best friend Lane Cutler and if I get to him before these two do then I will shoot him down like the mad dog he is.'

He pushed Joe Quillan in the chest and moved away. Suddenly the old man let out a grunt of scorn.

'You talk big, sonny. But you know nothing. That friend of yours, the young deputy, he got what was coming to him. He was a cold killer who shot a man in the back. He killed my son. Vince's brother.'

13

He was tired and hungry and his mood was sour. He felt as though the time was right to walk away and return to the family home further north. The war had been over for more than a year and things were returning to normal in Kansas and his father and brother would be pushing ahead with their expansion plans for the Bar-Q, plans that included extending the ranch until it was the biggest spread in the territory.

But Matt Quillan felt a sense of loyalty to the man now sleeping soundly near the dying embers of their campfire. Ray Calhoun's brother Brad had been gone for more than a month and, with his mother so seriously sick that the doctor did not hold out any hope other than prayer that she might survive the illness; old man Calhoun had sent his younger son in search of his brother, who had left to join a cattle drive heading for Dodge City.

Matt had volunteered to join his young friend, but for more than a week they had been out of luck. Reaching the drovers' camp they discovered that Brad Calhoun had quit after only three days, giving the trail boss no reason for his decision. The boss had been unwilling to help find a man who had run out on him with the job barely under way, but further questioning elicited enough information to give them a trail to follow. But here they were, three days later and still no sign of the missing brother.

Matt settled down for the night after coming to the decision that he had been reluctant to reach: tomorrow he would persuade his friend that to carry on the search was pointless and they would be better heading back to the Calhoun place.

But a good night's sleep freshened his mind and by morning his mood had changed. They would go on and he would help Ray find his brother. Because that was what friends did.

They drove their horses hard and stopped only to replenish their supplies and rest the tired animals. The days passed but still Brad's whereabouts eluded them.

On the eighth day they reached the ridge above the small farm.

'Looks like a good spot to water the horses and stock up on some food,' Ray suggested.

'Right, so let's not linger,' Matt agreed. The two riders dug in their heels and headed down the hill towards the workman who was fixing a broken-down wagon.

Looking up, the man threw down his hammer and raced towards the house. Off to his left, close to a small corral, a young boy turned his attention to the oncoming riders.

They were still some thirty yards from the water trough when the first shot rang out. It came from a rifle fired from inside the house and although the bullet whistled over Ray Calhoun's head it forced the two to leap from their saddles and head for the cover of a deserted barn.

'What the hell was that for?' Matt yelled.

'Don't know, but it looks like we've come at a bad time,' Ray answered with a grin.

Another gunshot sounded, this time ripping through the rotting woodwork above his head . . . then came a third.

'I reckon we're not welcome, Matt,' Calhoun suggested. 'I think we should get the hell out of here.'

They headed for their horses at a crouching, weaving run. Suddenly, Matt realized that the shooting had stopped. Pausing, he ducked behind a rock and watched as the boy raced into the house while a man — presumably the one who had done the shooting — whipped his horse into a gallop and headed off into the distance.

'Come on, Matt!' Ray was already mounted and urging his horse forward.

Together the pair raced past the house and headed off in the direction the man from the house had taken, but by the time they reached the foot of the slope he was out of sight. The horizon was empty. Another rifle shot came from the veranda of the house.

Reaching the top of the rise, Ray slowed to wait for his friend to reach him. To his horror, he saw that his friend's horse had come almost to a standstill. Matt was slumped forward over the horn of his saddle.

'Oh, God!'

Calhoun dismounted and rushed across to his friend. A close examination confirmed that Matt Quillan had been hit in the back, just below the left shoulder blade.

'Easy, Matt,' Ray urged, reaching up to examine the bullet wound. He said nothing but he knew it looked bad for his friend. He had to get him to a doctor and quick — though he knew enough to realize that if he rushed it would only hasten the flow of blood.

After applying a makeshift padding in an attempt to stanch the flow, Ray remounted, took the reins of Matt's horse and rode over the ridge, down into the valley on the other side.

It was a long slow ride before they eventually reached the outbuildings leading to the town of Redwood. Ray checked for the fifth time that his friend was still alive. Matt was fading fast when Ray called on the help of two men leaving the saloon. They helped Matt into the doc's while Ray headed inside the saloon for a drink that would calm him before he followed them.

He was still staring blankly into the empty beer glass when a hand touched his shoulder. He turned to look into the face of one of the men who had helped him with Matt. He was wearing a sheriff's badge.

'I think you ought to tell me what happened, son. I'm sorry to have to tell you — your friend just died.'

14

'That's a filthy lie!'

Corey Hayes hurled himself at the old man, knocking him to the floor before Ben or Tommy Kane could react. The pair crashed against the table and sent it spinning against a wall.

'You lying piece of — '

Corey felt an arm wrap around his throat as he was dragged off the startled rancher, who was gasping for breath.

'Are you crazy, Corey?' The anger in Ben's question stunned the young deputy but he shook himself free and turned on the marshal.

'He's lying, Ben. His son was a bounty hunter and he was chasing Lane's father when he got himself killed. Lane was only doing what any son would have done.'

Tommy helped Joe Quillan to his feet and settled him into a chair.

'What do you say to that, Mr Quillan?'

The old man was still trying to recover from the surprise attack but when he eventually managed to speak nobody interrupted.

'I — I'm not lying, Marshal. I may have done a lot of things that could get me inside your jail or maybe even at the end a rope but if there's been one good thing in my life it was my son Matthew. Sure, he took after his mother but he was a good son. He wasn't a bounty hunter. He was helping a friend find his brother. That's the truth and Lane Cutler shot him in the back. It was just how Ray Calhoun told me.'

He paused and reached for a drink.

'Cutler got what he deserved,' he muttered almost under his breath.

'And what about Sam Duncan? And Luther Bush? And George Benson?'

It was Ben McCabe who stood and posed the question.

Quillan sighed. 'I'm sorry about George,' he said, 'but not the others.

They knew what they were getting into, Marshal. They made a lot of money out of me.'

He took another long drink and sighed again. His time was over. His wife and young son were dead; his elder son was on the run for murder and his sight was failing fast. It was time to let go, to tell the marshal what he wanted to know. But he would not give up Vince. He could not do that, even if he could tell McCabe that his son was a killer. The lawman already knew that. He fumbled for his whiskey glass, refilled it and offered drinks around. Nobody accepted.

'I had known Luther Bush since we fought together in the Mexican War as Texas Rangers and if we overstepped the mark a few times, well, we were at war. Looting was rife.'

He paused and strained his eyes to look into the faces of his visitors. Then he smiled.

'Don't look so shocked, Marshal. I'm not telling you anything that you didn't already guess. Not if you've been listening to Luther. He was the one who gave you my name: he told me that much. Oh, he came over all sorry but did you know he was planning to run out on me, taking the gold with him? We did well out of the '49 gold rush in California, Marshal, though I can't say it was all the profit of hard work. It seemed easier to let somebody else do the digging.'

'What is this, Joe? Confession is good for the soul?'

As an answer, the old man reached inside a desk drawer and withdrew a sheet of paper, which he handed to Ben. The marshal unfolded it and read: WANTED FOR GOLD ROBBERY — JACK QUADE (alias JOE QUILLAN) and GANG. $1,000 REWARD.

Underneath there was a description that would have clearly applied to a young Joe Quillan and, unless Ben was mistaken, Luther Bush among others.

'Keeping it as a reminder of those days, eh?'

'My final link with those days, Marshal.'

'So you got rid of Luther because he was running out on you?' Tommy put in. 'What about Sam Duncan?'

'Sam was getting greedy. He kept quiet about what he knew just so long as the paying went on. Then when he told us that your new deputy was the kid who killed Matthew, Vince and I came up with the plan that would let us get rid of both of them.' He chuckled before continuing: 'It was Luther's idea to put the deputy's badge in Sam's hand just to add a bit more evidence.'

'You went to a lot of trouble.'

Joe Quillan shrugged.

'I could have shot him in the back — just like he did to my son. But that was too easy. I wanted him to suffer.'

He told them how he had taken Lane prisoner, sent Zak Hardin into town in Cutler's clothes with a message for Duncan and instructions to make sure that he was seen.

It was Hardin who burned down the

newspaper office and shot Duncan; and it was Hardin and another of the Bar-Q hands who killed Luther.

McCabe did not need to be told who had arranged — maybe even carried out — the hanging of Lane Cutler.

'So who told Vince where he could find Lane?' Ben asked.

Quillan scoffed. 'You think Vince hanged that young killer? Then you're a fool, McCabe. I didn't need my son's help to put a rope round Cutler's neck once Lennon had told me where you were hiding him. I did it and I ain't ashamed of doing what any judge would have ordered.'

Ben knew that was a lie. This man was too old, too frail to hang a healthy young man without help.

'And what about George Benson? Did you kill him as well?'

'No. Like I said, I'm sorry about George; he was family.'

'So that must have been Vince,' McCabe said. 'Just a harmless old man who wanted to sell up and join his daughter. He knew nothing about any of this. Where is Vince, Joe?'

'And where's Hardin?' Tommy put in.

The old man shrugged. 'I've told you all I know.'

'We'll find him and when we do there'll probably be gunplay. He's already a killer, and — '

'If what you say is true,' said Quillan, 'then his only chance is to get as far away from here as he can. You've already decided that he killed that man in the saloon.'

'And George Benson,' Ben reminded him. 'There's been too much killing these past few days and they all point back to the Bar-Q.' He turned to Corey. 'I want you to take Joe back to Progress and make him comfortable in a cell till we get back, with — or without — Vince.'

Corey nodded.

'I'd be glad to, Marshal.'

He pulled Quillan to his feet and rough-handled him towards the door.

He was in no mood to go easy on the man who had killed his friend. But when they reached the veranda the old man suddenly stopped in his tracks.

'Just a minute, son. Tell me what you see out there.'

Puzzled, Corey stared into the distance.

'What can I see? I can see what you can see — cattle grazing, a couple of horses wandering loose and far too much land for any one man.'

'And the hills?' Joe queried.

'What about the hills?'

'Is there any snow on them, yet?'

'Snow? There's no snow on them; you can see for yourself there's no snow.'

Joe turned towards the young deputy.

'That's just it, son. I can't see. I'm almost blind, so there's nothing you can do to me that will persuade me to hand over my son.'

★ ★ ★

Dan Hooper had been around cattle all his life, from the day his family bought a small ranch in Oklahoma. From there he had moved on to join the cattle drives north from Texas, eventually manning the chuck wagons after a stampede injury forced him out of the drover's saddle for the last time.

His cooking had not improved over the years, but he had somehow managed to persuade Joe Quillan that he could satisfy the taste buds and appetites of a few ranch hands as well as carry out the odd job around the Bar-Q.

He always assumed that Mr Quillan had looked upon him as a charity case — and Joe wasn't given to regular displays of good will — but Dan reckoned he had done enough to earn his keep in the five years he had been at the Bar-Q.

He was fixing a broken bar on the corral gate when he observed the arrival of the three riders. They had been inside the house for less than thirty minutes when Quillan emerged, ahead of the youngest lawman. They stood on the veranda for a few moments and appeared to be looking over the scene. Then, to Dan's astonishment, he watched the young deputy tie the old man's hands together and help him into the saddle.

It was as clear as day: Joe Quillan was under arrest.

Dan threw aside his hammer, pulled off his heavy gloves, and although limping badly, the handicap from that fall many years earlier, hurried towards the departing pair.

His voice, husky from too many years swallowing trail dust, was scarcely above a whisper as he reached the two riders.

'What's happening, Mr Quillan? How come you're all tied up like that? Where's he takin' you?'

Quillan leaned over.

'Don't worry, Dan. Just a little local difficulty in Progress. But you can do me one favour, friend.'

'Sure, Mr Quillan. Anything.'

'If you see Vince, tell him Marshal McCabe wants to see him and Zak.'

'Will do, boss. Will they know what it's about?'

'He'll know, Dan. They'll both know.'

Quillan felt a tug on his reins.

'Come on, we've got a long ride ahead,' Corey snapped.

★ ★ ★

Zak Hardin cursed the day he had arrived at the Bar-Q and taken on the job of nursemaid to Vince Quillan. As if he did not have enough troubles of his own.

Old Joe had convinced him that there was no safer place to hide from the law than in full view.

'They never look right under their noses,' he had told him. 'And who would look for a wanted cattle rustler in a bunch of cowhands?'

So he had taken the job and because Quillan knew all about him from the

Wanted bills he kept in his desk, the instructions came to keep Vince out of trouble.

At first he had done his best, but as the months passed he began to envy Vince and his wild spirit. Zak had been that way once, living life according to his own rules. Vince, though, had no rules and Hardin could see the benefits of that. He went where he wanted, when he wanted, and all the time Zak had to tag along just to make sure that the boss's son stayed out of trouble.

Except for the occasional saloon-bar brawl and the attentions of an angry husband, he had done the job well . . . until the old man offered him a $2,000 bonus to burn down the newspaper office.

'The place will be empty. All you have to do is put a torch to it and get the hell out of there fast.'

No questions — just get the job done and get out!

But there was somebody in there. A body. A body with a bullet in his back.

So he had lit the torch and hidden in the shadows with Vince at his side while the frantic townspeople of Progress tried in vain to put out the flames.

But that had only been the start. It was followed by the killing of Luther Bush, for what Joe Quillan said was betrayal but Zak knew was all about the gold, and George Benson, for no reason that Zak could imagine. And now this, Vince sitting opposite him outside an old, abandoned stage station, telling him how he had to get away because he had killed a man over a card game in Progress. But even worse, he had killed Jed Lennon, for no better reason than that he wanted to see his old man's spy squirm.

'You're a crazy fool, Vince. What the hell were you thinking about, going into Progress? How can I help you now? And why should I? If the old man found out he'd — '

Vince spat into the dust.

'He'll do nothing,' he said sourly, his voice full of spite. 'He already knows. I told him last night.'

Hardin groaned. He was close to despair. Sure, he had made plenty of money on the back of Joe Quillan and the Bar-Q and no lawman had come looking for him in the past three years. But Vince was wild and dangerous. He was out of control.

'You just have to get away, as far and as fast as that nag will take you,' Zak urged.

But Vince was not listening. He got to his feet and wandered away, deep in thought. Suddenly he turned on the ranch foreman.

'I'm going nowhere till I get what's mine.'

'Yours? What the hell is yours?'

'The gold. That gold you and Jake took from the mayor after you'd beaten him to death.'

'Man, you are crazy. That will be locked away in the vaults in the Progress Bank.'

'No it ain't. It's still in the house. In the safe. The old man has never trusted banks.' Vince laughed. 'He robbed too many in the old days to trust them.'

Hardin drew heavily on a cheroot. Vince might be a loose cannon, but if what he said was true and the gold was still at the house it would be the easiest job he had ever had, just to walk in and take it.

'After that we'll be free of the Bar-Q. We can go our own ways. And you know what that means to me, Zak. I got big plans for me and Mary. California, maybe. Or Oregon. Leastways I'm out of there. My pa hasn't been the same since Matt was killed five, six years back. I thought maybe after I'd strung up that Lane Cutler kid things would change. Maybe he would look at me differently. But he's just the same. Even when I told him I had got rid of that crazy Mexican who was cheating him every time he went into town for supplies he wasn't happy. He said I was a fool. Just like you did, Zak. You said I was a crazy fool.'

Vince's staring blue eyes were as cold

as ice. 'You still think I'm a fool?'

He was toying with his gun, spinning the barrel and twirling it around his finger like some showman. This was no time to cross Vince, so Zak laughed half-heartedly. Almost apologetic.

'A bit wild maybe, Vince. But crazy? I've tangled with worse.'

Vince holstered his gun.

'Then I reckon we should get back to the house before you change your mind again.'

They had a two-hour ride ahead of them — plenty of time for Zak to develop a plan that was already beginning to form in his head.

And it did not include Vince Quillan. Vince may have thought he had only to ride into St Joseph to pick up his woman and ride out again. But it wasn't going to be that easy. Mary Seabrooke was a good-looking woman, sure enough, and her dalliance with Vince had been ammunition for the men at the Bar-Q; but Zak reckoned, like the rest, that it wouldn't ever become a permanent arrangement.

Even old Joe would not stand by a son who planned to rob him of all he owned to save his own skin. If Zak played his cards right the Bar-Q would be his one day. All he had to do was to show the old man that he was the sort of son that Vince could never be. Loyal.

As the pair rode in silence across the fertile grazing ground that formed part of the western side of the Bar-Q, Zak had the feeling that life was about to change for ever.

★ ★ ★

Joe Quillan sank low in the saddle. His hands were tied in front of him, his head bowed. The richest ranch owner in the territory was a beaten man. Behind him was the Bar-Q, the ranch that had become his life; ahead lay the town of Progress, where that life could end in a jail cell.

The young deputy who had been his escort for more than three hours had not said a word, even when they had stopped to rest the horses. Joe had tried to look into the man's face but could see nothing other than contempt. After all, he had confessed to killing the boy's friend — even if that confession had been a complete lie. But time was running out and his chances of buying his way to freedom were disappearing.

'Tell me about your friend,' he said at last.

'You killed him,' Corey snapped. 'That's all you need to know.'

Joe Quillan persisted. 'Even so, I'd like to hear about him. You said he thought Matt . . . my son . . . was a bounty hunter. Why would a bounty hunter go after your friend's father?'

Corey was silent. All he had ever known about Bob Cutler was what Lane had told him and that was very little. Cutler had spent more time away from home than with his family.

'Tell me,' the old man insisted.

'I've got nothing to say that will help you,' Corey answered.

They moved ever closer to the

boundaries of Progress. Then Quillan spoke again.

'I'm sorry . . . about your friend. But he did kill my son.'

Suddenly Corey pulled the horses to a halt and turned to face his prisoner.

'And you lynched him from a tree without a trial, without any explanation. Without even trying to find out what happened. You're a killer, old man, and you'll hang . . . only it will be all legal and not in some out-of-the-way scrub to be left hanging like rotting meat.'

'And that will make you feel better?' Quillan asked. 'I mean, hanging an old man who's going blind but who killed out of grief for the loss of his son. Is that what you want? Will that bring your friend back?'

Corey didn't answer. He had come to Progress to help find Lane's killer and now he had him. But was Quillan right? Was this all about vengeance ahead of justice? And would there be any satisfaction in seeing a frail, nearly blind man led up to a scaffold to hang?

Lane was dead, killed because he tried to defend his father — a man wanted by the law. Was this old man guilty of anything worse?

He was hardly listening when Quillan suddenly said: 'I'm a rich man, Deputy. And I could make you rich.'

He paused and waited for a reply but when none came he hurried on: 'All you have to do is untie these ropes and let me ride off out of here. You could always say I took you by surprise. You weren't expecting an old man to jump you. Does that sound like a bad deal?'

Corey made a pretence of thinking it over. Then he said: 'Tell me something — would you make the same offer to Marshal McCabe?'

Without waiting for a reply, Corey tugged at the reins of Quillan's horse and stepped up the pace towards the town.

15

Ben McCabe and Tommy Kane spread their search far and wide across the vast expanse that was the Bar-Q ranch, but by late afternoon there had been no signs of either Vince Quillan or Zak Hardin. The lawmen had come across several ranch hands but none had known the whereabouts of either the foreman or the owner's son.

'We're not the most welcome visitors in these parts,' Ben reflected as the two men turned back towards the big house. 'I don't reckon we would have got the truth out of any of them even if we had held a gun to their heads.'

'Could be they are well out of the state by now,' said Tommy. 'But at least you've got the old man locked away back in Progress.'

'It wasn't Joe who killed old Fred

Adams. It was Vince. And I want Vince to pay for it.'

The pair rode on in silence for several minutes before Tommy suddenly held up his hand and pointed towards a cloud of dust in the distance. Even in the fading sunlight they were able to make out a buckboard and its single driver.

'He looks to be in a hurry to get someplace,' Ben suggested.

'Let's see where that is,' Tommy answered. He dug in his heels and turned his mount towards the distant dust.

Up ahead Dan Hooper failed to notice the two riders who had suddenly started to follow him. He had his mind on other things. Joe Quillan had told him to let Vince know that the marshal wanted to see him, and in Dan's mind that meant only one thing. The son was in trouble with the law.

Joe had been good to him so Dan felt he owed the family. Not Vince, because he was not worth the trouble, but Joe had asked him as a personal favour. Vince had not returned throughout the day, so Dan decided that he must have been hiding out. And Dan had been around long enough and listened to enough gossip among the ranch hands to know the kind of place Vince would head for.

The old disused stage station on the edge of the ranch's southern pastures was a safe place for anybody on the run.

The two lawmen followed the buckboard for three miles, keeping their distance until the driver steered his way out of sight behind a rocky butte. He re-emerged in a clearing, pulling to a halt alongside the abandoned staging post. Leaning forward in the saddle, Ben studied the scene below.

'That's old Dan Hooper. I've seen him about town a few times collecting supplies for the Bar-Q. What's he doing all the way out here?'

'Let's see,' Tommy answered, nudging his horse forward.

Hooper climbed down from the buckboard and hurried inside. Within seconds he was out again. The place was deserted. He stood for a moment, baffled by the absence of any signs of Vince's ever having been there. He was climbing back on to the buckboard when the two lawmen appeared on the hillside. He did not need to think long and hard why they were there. He waited for the two men to pull up.

'You been following me, Marshal?'

'That's right, Dan. We saw you lashing the hide of that horse as though you were in one hell of a hurry to get somewhere. Like you had a message to deliver.'

'Then it looks like you're out of luck. As you can see, there's nobody here. And if it's Vince you're wanting then I can't help you. He ain't here.'

'Which means he is hiding out somewhere else,' Tommy put in, his voice heavy with scorn. 'And you're going to tell us where that might be.'

'If I knew that, mister, I wouldn't be

out here looking for him, would I?'

'He's a killer, Dan,' Ben said quietly.

Hooper tried to look puzzled. He had always known Vince was no good but he was not going to be the one to hand him over to the law.

'Then I reckon you ought to go and find him, Marshal. I've got some cooking to do for the ranch hands. Mr Quillan wouldn't want me neglecting his men while he sorts out that little difficulty in Progress.'

He climbed on to the buckboard, spun the horse around and headed for the ranch house. He did not say anything about the note he had left, a precaution in case, as indeed happened, his search for Vince had been in vain.

* * *

An hour's ride away, Vince and Zak Hardin dismounted outside the main house, which was in semi-darkness. Inside, Vince headed for the big desk where he knew his father kept the key to the safe. On top of the desk he found the scribbled note left by Dan Hooper, warning him that the marshal was looking for him and that his father had been taken to Progress by a deputy.

He screwed up the paper and threw it into the basket at the side of the desk. What did he care? He knew what he wanted and where to get it: the gold and as much money as he could carry. Joe Quillan could buy his way out of the trouble he was in. It had never failed him before.

'The old man must have turned in,' Vince suggested. 'That will make things a lot easier.'

And quicker, thought Zak. The sooner they emptied the safe the sooner he could play his part in the drama he had rehearsed in his head. He would help Vince to load up with the gold and the cash from the safe and then, when they were out on the open road, he would slug him from behind and drag him back to the house, exposing him to his father as a thief and a killer. Even

Joe Quillan would wash his hands of his son after that.

Fumbling in the gathering darkness, Vince headed for the safe and the gold he knew had come from his father's days as a renegade soldier in California, before he was born. Stuffing his saddle-bags, Vince barked his orders to Hardin.

'Check upstairs while I load the horses,' he snapped. 'We don't want the old man waking up and finding us here.'

The foreman didn't argue. Quietly making his way up the staircase, he was still thinking ahead, chewing over the plan he had formed to take care of Vince once and for all. But, as the foreman was making his way to the room at the far end of the corridor, Vince had other ideas.

By the time Zak had checked on the old man he would be out of there. If he was followed he would deal with it, and one day Zak Hardin's body would be a welcome sight for the buzzards.

* * *

The town of Progress was quiet. Even the Silver Spur saloon was in semi-darkness as only a handful of drinkers were scattered around the room. Nobody sat at the piano and the two saloon girls were already showing signs of boredom, hinting to the barman that they were wasting their time and they could be better employed back at the hotel.

In the marshal's office across the street things were not so quiet. Ben McCabe was angry.

'He's lying,' he said for the third time. 'He couldn't have killed Lane and the others — at least not without a lot of help.'

Joe Quillan was locked away in a cell at the back of the building while in the front room of the office Ben, Tommy Kane and Corey Hayes were recounting the day's events.

'Vince is out there somewhere and until we find him the old man will stick to his story — that he killed Lane and

252

some hired guns shot Luther Bush and George Benson.'

Tommy got up from his seat and strolled across the room.

'We're going round in circles, Ben. We've been looking for Vince all day. If he's got any sense he will be out of the territory — maybe even out of the state by now. He could even be headed for Mexico.'

'Maybe,' Ben mused. 'But if he's the sort of man we think he is he won't be going empty-handed.'

'The gold,' Corey interrupted. 'That means he has to go back to the house. We should have waited there. He would have walked right into our hands.'

Ben nodded. 'That makes sense. If we leave at first light tomorrow he'll have a day's start on us and we don't know where he is headed. But we do know somebody who might.'

An hour later Joe Quillan at last told the marshal what he wanted to know.

'He needed some persuading,' Ben told the others when he returned from the cell. 'It seems even Joe Quillan's fatherly love doesn't stretch as far as his love for gold and money.

'Maybe I had to elaborate on what we really know, but when I told the old man that we knew that Vince had run out with everything he could carry from the house, he told me what I wanted to know. Vince will be in St Joseph, Missouri. But St Joe is a sizeable town. The old man says we'd never find Vince without his help, so he'll be coming along.'

'Why should we believe him?' Corey asked. 'He's done nothing but cheat and lie all his life.'

'I thought the same thing. But I believe him because of what he said. He's already told you, Corey, that he's going blind and he wants to see his son one more time before his sight gives out. That's good enough for me. And, Tommy, he reckons that wherever Vince goes, Zak Hardin will be with him. Tomorrow's going to be a busy day so I suggest we all get some sleep.'

Corey Hayes did not sleep that night. He did not even go back to his hotel room. Instead he decided that Ben McCabe was too much of a man of principle to give him what he had come to Progress for. The marshal wanted to take Vince Quillan alive.

But for Corey this was personal. An-eye-for-an-eye personal. He knew that the old man was covering for his son and that while Vince lived Lane Cutler's murder would be unavenged.

Corey left the marshal's office and walked his horse to the edge of the town. There he mounted up and rode off into the darkness.

St Joseph, Missouri was more than a day's ride and Corey needed a good start.

16

Zak Hardin eased open the bedroom door. One glance into the darkened room was not enough to reveal anything. It was only when he ventured inside that he discovered that the bed and the room were empty. He slammed the door behind him, hurried back to the passage and rushed back down the staircase.

Vince had gone.

Hardin cursed. The lamebrain had run out on him.

Racing towards the door, he knew that Vince could not have got far in the few minutes they had been out of each other's sight.

Out on the veranda he stared into the blackness. There was nothing to see. Night had closed in and a storm was not far away. Angrily, Zak unholstered his gun and fired twice into the sky.

'Damn you, Quillan. You lying, cheating — '

He stopped in mid-rant. Vince was out there. He couldn't see him. But he was there. Zak knew it.

'Running out on me, Vince?' he shouted at the darkness.

No reply.

'Get greedy, Vince? Is that it?' he yelled again.

This time he got his answer. A bullet smashed into the wooden framework close to his head. Then another — closer this time, ricocheting off the handrail. He dived for cover and fired back at an unseen target. Then there was silence, followed by the sound of galloping hoofs. Vince screamed an obscenity as he raced past, firing aimlessly towards the house while Hardin crouched behind the protection of the fencing.

He waited until Vince had vanished into the night before dashing across the yard to the corral where his horse was still saddled after the ride from the far side of the Bar-Q.

He mounted up, steered the horse out of the corral and headed away from the house. Already the rain was lashing into his face but he knew what he had to do. He could not let Vince get away. He knew where he would find him. St Joe was a large town but Zak knew where he would be. But he didn't know that he was not the only rider braving the storm that night, nor that by the following morning there would be three others on the road, to cross the Missouri River into St Joseph.

* * *

Corey was wet and tired and the storm had taken a lot out of his horse. It was time to rest up and finish the ride the following morning. A rest would give him the chance to devise his plan for dealing with the man who had killed his friend.

Marshal Ben McCabe had had his chance. Now it was time to do the right thing by Lane.

He knew that the badge he was wearing would give him no authority in the state of Missouri, and St Joseph was nothing like the outback towns of Progress and Redwood where he had been brought up. He could hardly walk into the nearest saloon and expect Vince to be standing at the bar waiting for a shoot-out. He would have to be careful.

He still had not formed a clear plan when he eventually fell asleep just before dawn.

* * *

Ben McCabe was angry again. He had called at the boarding house where he had expected to collect Corey for the ride north, only to find that his young deputy had not been in his room. Judging by the state of the place he had not been there all night. Which meant only one thing: he was already on his way to Missouri to track down Vince Quillan.

When he arrived at the jailhouse, Tommy Kane was already waiting, with Joe Quillan pacing his cell floor.

'It means we're in for a hard ride, Ben,' Tommy said when he was told of Corey's absence. 'If the kid gets there ahead of us he'll shoot first and ask questions when it's too late.'

Ben did not want to believe that, but there was no escaping the fact that if Corey had simply wanted to bring Vince in for a trial he would have waited. Now he was out there . . . somewhere . . . with only one thing on his mind. Revenge for the killing of his friend. As Ben led the trio out of town he knew that he had to find Corey Hayes before it was too late.

*   *   *

The Patee Hotel, a four-storey brick building that rose above the rest of the St Joseph skyline, was a popular place for Missouri businessmen. It was also the chosen meeting point for Vince Quillan and the wife of railroad executive

Marston Seabrooke.

If there were times in his life when Vince was not the heartless, cold-blooded killer without a thought for anybody, they came when he was in the company of Mary Seabrooke. She knew nothing of his life in neighbouring Kansas other than what he had told her. That he was the only son of a rich ranch owner and he would soon be in a position to offer her a life away from her loud-mouthed, bullying husband. A new life in California. That was what she wanted and Vince was the man to provide it.

What she did not know about his past did not concern her, so when the young messenger delivered the hand-written note that contained the news she had been waiting for, she felt a surge of excitement running through her body.

Shortly after midday she entered the hotel and made her way up the stairs to the room that had been her secret meeting place for the past few months.

As she knew he would be, Vince was waiting for her.

They embraced, long and hard, and it was only when she pushed him gently away and stared lovingly into his face that Vince, gambler, killer and regular drunkard, spoke softly. When he had finished speaking, he nodded in the direction of the saddle-bags hooked over the corner of the bed.

'In those bags, Mary, there's almost a hundred thousand dollars in gold, bonds and cash — enough to set us up in California for the rest of our lives.'

She did not ask how he had come by such riches: she did not want to know. What she did know was that the time had come to make her decision. Should she leave her husband and head for California with her lover? She hesitated only for a moment. A glance in the direction of the saddle-bags convinced her.

She was still a young woman, not yet out of her twenties, and the thought of spending the rest of her life under the choking power of her aggressive husband was all she needed. Reaching out, she took Vince's hand and led him across the room to the bed, pulling him down on top of her.

An hour later they dressed, and headed towards the stairs.

They had just reached the steps of the hotel when he suddenly froze in mid-stride. Marching across the street in the direction of the hotel was the last man in the world he wanted to see.

Zak Hardin was heading his way.

17

'Running out on me again, Vince?'

'Zak!'

Vince felt the tug on his arm and turned to see the look of alarm in Mary's eyes. He smiled at her but there was no conviction in it.

'Mary — this is Zak Hardin, my father's ranch foreman.'

'Hah!' Hardin scoffed. 'Is that all I am, Vince? Just your old man's foreman? After all we've been through together don't you think I deserve more than that?'

'What's he saying, Vince? What does he mean — all you've been through?'

Vince took the woman's arm and led her out of earshot of the Bar-Q ranch man.

'Listen, darling, it looks as though we may have to put off our trip for an hour or two. You go back up to the hotel room. Take these bags back upstairs and I'll be along as soon as I can sort out Zak's problem.'

Reluctantly, Mary Seabrooke went back into the hotel and watched the two men cross the street to the saloon.

But she was not the only person watching when the two men entered the bar. Corey Hayes stepped out of the shadows thrown by the overhang along the sidewalk and slipped down a side alley.

* * *

Five miles outside St Joseph, Ben McCabe, Tommy Kane and Joe Quillan slowed their tired horses to a walk.

The old man spoke, to end a silence that had lasted for more than an hour.

'You've got to let me talk to Vince, Marshal. You got to let me try to talk him into coming back to face trial.'

Ben drew up alongside the rancher.

'I made no promises, Joe, except to let you see your son before we bring him in. Whether he comes without gunplay is up to him. You know him better than I do and he's killed before, so I'm expecting him to shoot his way out.'

Joe Quillan mopped his brow.

'St Joseph isn't still some frontier town where you can walk down Main Street and shoot it out,' he said with an air of desperation. 'You have to let me talk to Vince.'

Without answering, Ben edged his horse forward to where Tommy Kane had stopped.

Tommy shrugged and grinned. 'I'm here for Hardin, Ben. Vince Quillan's your problem.'

'Thanks, friend,' Ben said and turned his horse towards town.

It was true what Joe Quillan had said: St Joseph was not like Progress. Even with the marshal's badge on his chest Ben knew he could not ride into town and drag Vince out without the support of the Missouri law.

He had brought the old man along

because he thought he might need him to chase down Vince in a town of some 20,000 people. According to Joe there was only one reason for his son to make regular visits to the border town. A woman.

Joe had used the information given to him by Zak: that Vince's woman was Mary Seabrooke, wife of a railroad executive. They met in the Patee Hotel while Zak was made to wait in the saloon across the street.

'They couldn't be seen in town, Marshal,' Joe had told him. 'It seems the woman's husband, Marston Seabrooke, is a high rider in St Joseph and even my son wouldn't be stupid enough to risk a bullet for a woman.'

An hour later they reached the outskirts of town.

* * *

Vince Quillan toyed with his third whiskey. He still had not decided how he was going to deal with Zak. Maybe he could get him drunk enough to dump him in some alley. Or maybe he could promise him a share of the gold he had taken from his father's safe — a promise he would never intend to keep. He dismissed both thoughts almost at once. He knew there was only one way this could end. He could not let the foreman come between him and his plan to take Mary Seabrooke to a new life in California.

Zak broke a lengthy silence when he slammed his empty glass on to the table.

'You owe me, Vince. You and the old man,' he said with rising anger.

It was the opening Vince had been hoping for. A reason to fight.

'You've been well paid, Zak. We owe you nothing.'

Hardin filled his glass.

'I've been your friend and nursemaid for the last three years, keeping you out of jail, paying off your card debts, saving you from a bullet in the back — '

'And reporting everything to the old

man,' Vince snapped. 'Even Mary and me. From the day I started seeing her. You're no friend of mine, Hardin. You're the hired help, just like everybody else at the Bar-Q, and that gutless lot in Progress like Jed Lennon and that miserable mayor. The old man only kept you on because of me. Like I said, I owe you nothing.'

He moved to get up from his chair but Zak reached across the table and grabbed his shirt, pulling him down.

'I aim to get what's mine, Vince. We'll see what your father does when I get back to him and tell him what happened — how you emptied his safe and ran out on him.'

Vince gripped the other's wrist and shook himself free.

Sneering in the face of the Bar-Q foreman, Vince almost spat the words: 'Then I reckon you should get on your horse and head back to Progress. You'll find my father there, locked away in the town jail.'

Vince turned and marched out of the

saloon into the afternoon sun.

Open-mouthed, Zak watched him go before gulping down the rest of his drink and rushing out of the bar.

'Vince!' He yelled. 'Vince! Stop there! We ain't finished.'

Vince Quillan stopped in his tracks and turned.

The two men faced each other across the sun-drenched street.

* * *

Ben spotted them first. The three riders had just rounded the bend leading into the main street when the Progress lawman saw the duo who stood only a few paces apart in front of the saloon.

Pulling his horse to a halt, he turned to Tommy.

'Looks like we are both in luck. There they are, just waiting to be picked up.'

But it was Joe Quillan who reacted first. Without hesitating, he dug his heels into his horse and the animal bolted forward, reaching a gallop almost instantly.

Ahead of him, frightened pedestrians scattered for the protection of the sidewalks but Quillan did not seem to notice. His eyes were focused on his son and his foreman, who stood only a few paces apart. Even with his failing eyesight he could clearly make out the scene. It was one he had seen many times before and each time the result had been the same: a death on the street.

Clinging to the reins of his horse Joe Quillan closed in rapidly on the two men facing each other. The sound of pounding hoofs and the sight of the galloping horseman sent any still lingering pedestrians scattering for the cover of the stores and sidewalks.

In an instant the street was a scene of chaos . . . people dashing for cover, three riders closing in at speed and two angry men hell-bent on a showdown.

In a last desperate attempt to stop a shoot-out, Quillan charged his horse straight at Hardin. The Bar-Q foreman flung himself to his left, crashing into a disused hitching post. Searing pain ripped through his shoulder as he rolled screaming into the dust.

By the time Joe had pulled his horse to a halt Ben and Tommy Kane were already on the scene. Amid all the confusion Vince assessed his options. Even with Zak out of action the odds were still stacked against him — two armed lawmen against his single six-gun. And his father in the firing line.

Vince stood frozen to the spot. There was no place to go; nowhere to run. Even now it looked as though his own father had led the marshals to St Joseph.

'Unbuckle the gunbelt, Vince, and let it drop to the ground.' Ben dismounted and strolled over to retrieve the discarded belt. Across the street Tommy dragged his prisoner, Zak Hardin, to his feet.

Grim-faced, Joe Quillan looked on as his son's hands were tied behind him. What had he done? Why had he led McCabe and the other man straight to where he knew his son would be? Whatever Vince had done he was still his son. He had to know the truth.

He strode over, gripped Ben's arm and pulled him to one side.

'Marshal, I want to talk to my son. In private.'

Ben studied the old man's face. He was a broken figure, betrayed by his own flesh and blood, and he needed to know why. The chances were that both men would hang for murder and Ben at least owed him the chance to put things right between them.

'I'll give you two minutes,' Ben told him, 'but I'm staying in hearing distance, so don't try anything.'

Joe Quillan snorted. 'Like what, Marshal? His hands are tied and I'm an unarmed old man losing his sight.'

'You're using up your two minutes,' Ben said sourly and turned away.

An instant later the shot came. Ben spun round, his gun at the ready. His eyes scoured the street, then looked skywards. There it was, on the rooftop

273

of the three-storey building and glisten-
ing in the sunlight, the barrel of a rifle.
Firing upwards more in hope than judgement, Ben raced across the street and
leapt under the cover of the overhang.

Turning, he saw what he had feared.
Joe Quillan was kneeling over the body
of his son, Vince's head cradled in his
arms.

Ben rushed inside and found himself
in a deserted warehouse. In the semi-
darkness he could make out the staircase
to his left, leading up to a balcony.
Above that was another set of steps that
clearly led out on to the roof. Ben crept
stealthily up the staircase, keeping close
to the wall. He had no doubt who would
be waiting for him out on the roof and
he expected that only one of them would
be leaving the building alive.

Slowly making his way up the last
few steps, he pushed open the skylight
window and called out. There was no
answer. He tried again. More silence.

Slowly he let himself out on to the
rooftop. It was a risk but, if he was any

judge, it would be a small one. Once out in the open, a quick glance around told him that any danger had passed. The flat rooftop was deserted.

He walked to the back of the building and looked over the edge. An outside staircase led down to a yard at the rear. He turned, made his way to the front and stared out into the street below. A crowd had gathered and were clamouring for a view of the man lying dead in their midst. Ben was about to leave the roof and head back down the stairs when he spotted it, lying in the dust. Discarded, as if it was of no further use.

He bent down and picked it up, examining it closely before thrusting it into his shirt pocket. The deputy marshal's badge he had pinned on the young friend of Lane Cutler. Lane's killer was lying dead in the street and out there, heading towards the setting sun, was the man who had vowed to avenge his death. He watched the moving dust cloud gradually fade in the distance. He did not expect to see Corey Hayes again.

Ben McCabe was enjoying a quiet drink in the Patee Hotel when he was joined by Tommy Kane.

Zak Hardin and Joe Quillan were safely locked away in the custody of the St Joseph law officers for the night, while Vince's body had been taken to the undertaker's. He would later be moved for burial on the Bar-Q alongside his younger brother, but in the meantime Ben had his own problems to solve.

He had been a lawman for more than twenty years and he had done his share of rounding up the bad guys.

Times were changing; the railroad was spreading across the West and the law of the gun was becoming a thing of the past.

He was aroused from his musing by Tommy's arrival at the hotel.

The next hour was spent catching up on old times. By the time Tommy left, the pair had relived the years that had passed since they last met.

Alone again, Ben ordered a second drink, but before he could finish it he was interrupted again — this time by a pretty woman coming down the stairs of the hotel. She appeared to be struggling with her heavy baggage. Ben put down his beer glass and moved across to offer his help.

'Need a hand, miss?'

She smiled her thanks.

'That's very kind of you, mister, but I'm heading for the rail depot. I've got a buggy outside. If you could help me get this lot aboard I'd be very grateful.'

Ben lifted the heavy bag and threw the satchel over his shoulder.

'You going away for a spell?'

She smiled again.

'I've got a sister I haven't seen for a long time. How about you? I see you're a marshal. But not from these parts.'

They had reached the buggy and Ben had begun loading her luggage aboard before he answered.

'Well, as from now I'm no longer a marshal. When I get back to Progress

I'll be the proud owner of a small ranch. My business with the law ended out on the street this afternoon.'

'When that young man was killed? Yes, I saw that from my hotel room window. Who was he?'

Ben helped the woman on to her buggy.

'Not the sort of man a lady like you would want to know,' he said.

She smiled for the third time.

'If you say so, Marshal. Well, thanks for your help. And good luck with your ranch.'

Ben touched his hat. Mary Seabrooke set her buggy in motion and headed for the train.

THE END

We do hope that you have enjoyed reading this large print book.

Did you know that all of our titles are available for purchase?

We publish a wide range of high quality large print books including:
Romances, Mysteries, Classics
General Fiction
Non Fiction and Westerns

Special interest titles available in large print are:
The Little Oxford Dictionary
Music Book, Song Book
Hymn Book, Service Book

Also available from us courtesy of Oxford University Press:
Young Readers' Dictionary
(large print edition)
Young Readers' Thesaurus
(large print edition)

For further information or a free brochure, please contact us at:
Ulverscroft Large Print Books Ltd.,
The Green, Bradgate Road, Anstey,
Leicester, LE7 7FU, England.
Tel: (00 44) 0116 236 4325
Fax: (00 44) 0116 234 0205

Other titles in the
Linford Western Library:

DUEL OF THE OUTLAWS

John Russell Fearn

The inhabitants of Twin Pines, Arizona lead uneventful, happy lives — until the sudden arrival of Black Yankee and his gang. They shoot the sheriff, take over the place, and Twin Pines spirals downwards into an outlaw town, with lawlessness and sudden death the norm. When Thorn Tanworth, son of the sheriff, returns from his travels, to everyone's astonishment he establishes a mutually beneficial partnership with Black Yankee. But then the two men begin fighting each other for control of the town . . .

KID FURY

Michael D. George

The remote settlement of War Smoke lies quiet — until the calm is shattered by a gunshot. Marshal Matt Fallen and his deputy Elmer spring into action to investigate. Then another shot rings out, and cowboy Billy Jackson's horse gallops into town, dragging its owner's corpse in the dust: one boot still caught in its stirrup, and one hand gripping a smoking gun. Meanwhile, the paths of hired killer Waco Walt Dando and gunfighter Kid Fury are set to converge on War Smoke . . .

FIVE SHOTS LEFT

Ben Bridges

When you have only five shots left,
you have to make each one count. Like
the outlaw whose quest for revenge
didn't go quite according to plan. Or
the cowboy who ended up using a
most unusual weapon to defeat his
enemy. Then there was the store-
keeper who had to face his worst
fear. A down-at-heel sheepherder who
was obliged to set past hatreds aside
when renegade Comanches went on
the warpath. And an elderly couple
who struggled to keep the secret that
threatened to tear them apart . . .